The Children and the Whale

Daniel Frost

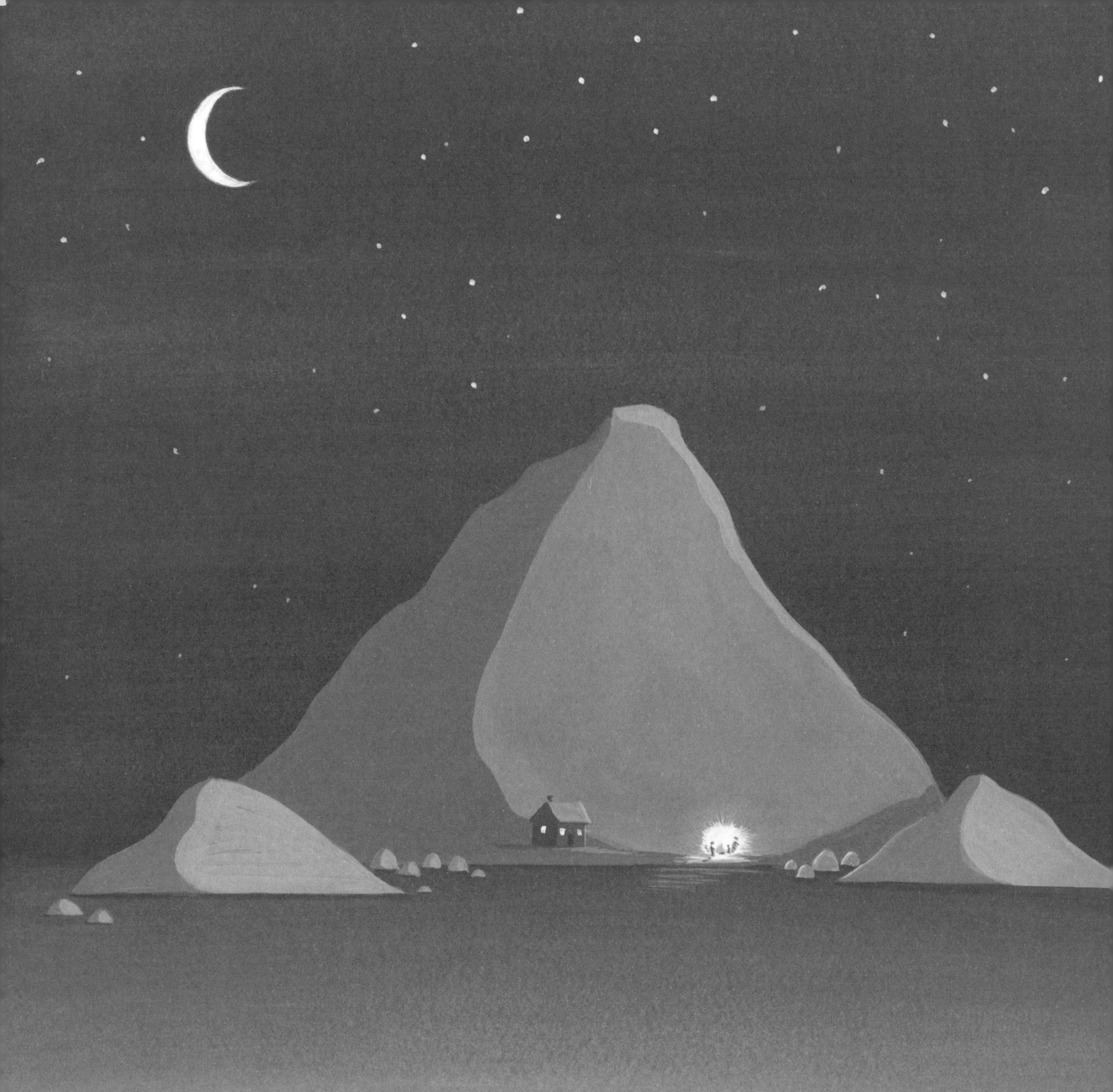

In the far, far north, Cuno and Aia gathered around a fire to hear their father's story. He told of a gigantic animal that once swam in the waters around their home.

"It is six times the size of our house. It has a heart as big as a boat and makes a noise that could break human bones," he growled.

"Have you seen it?" whispered Cuno excitedly.

"Not since I was your age," their father replied. "No one knows where the whale roams."

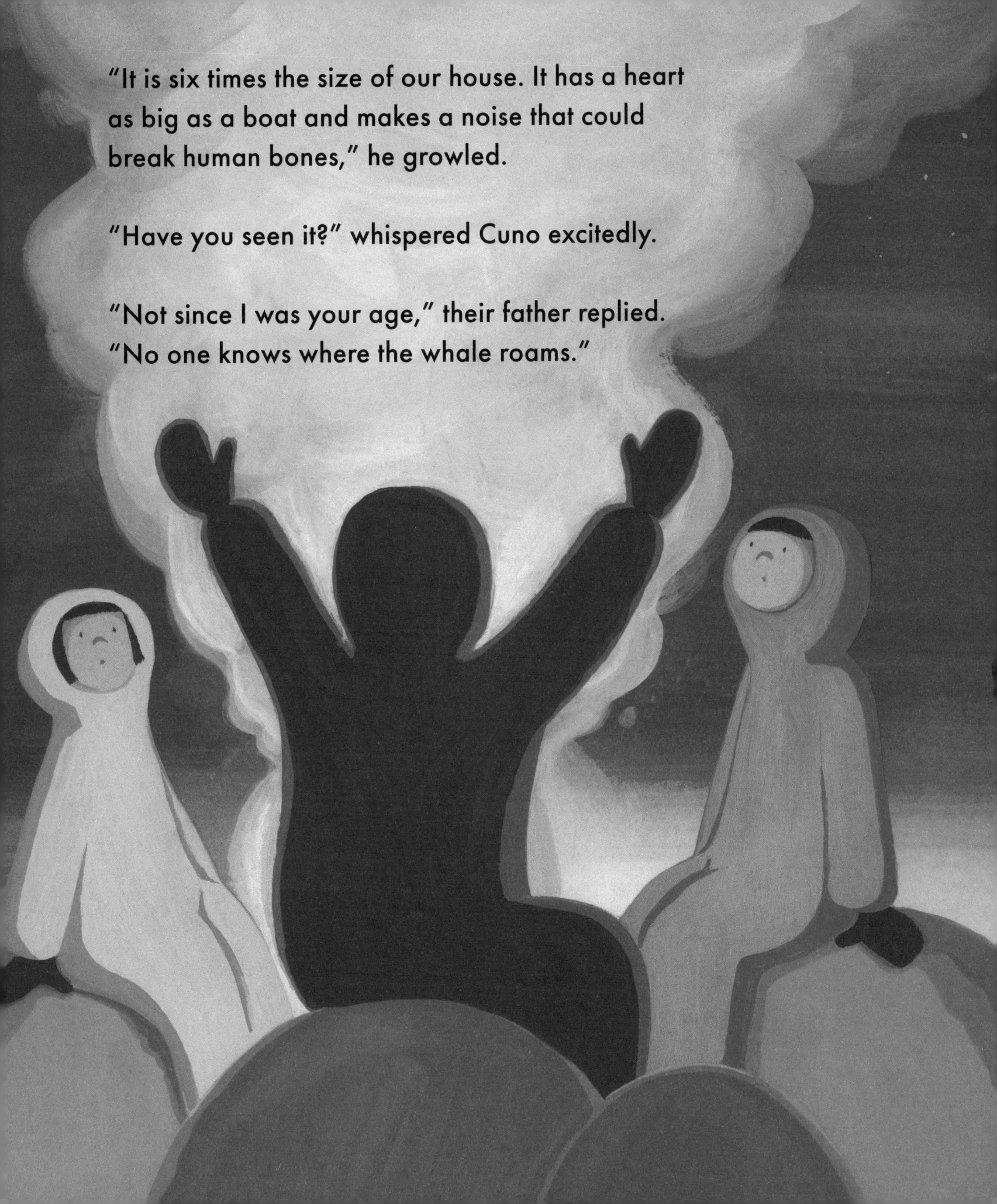

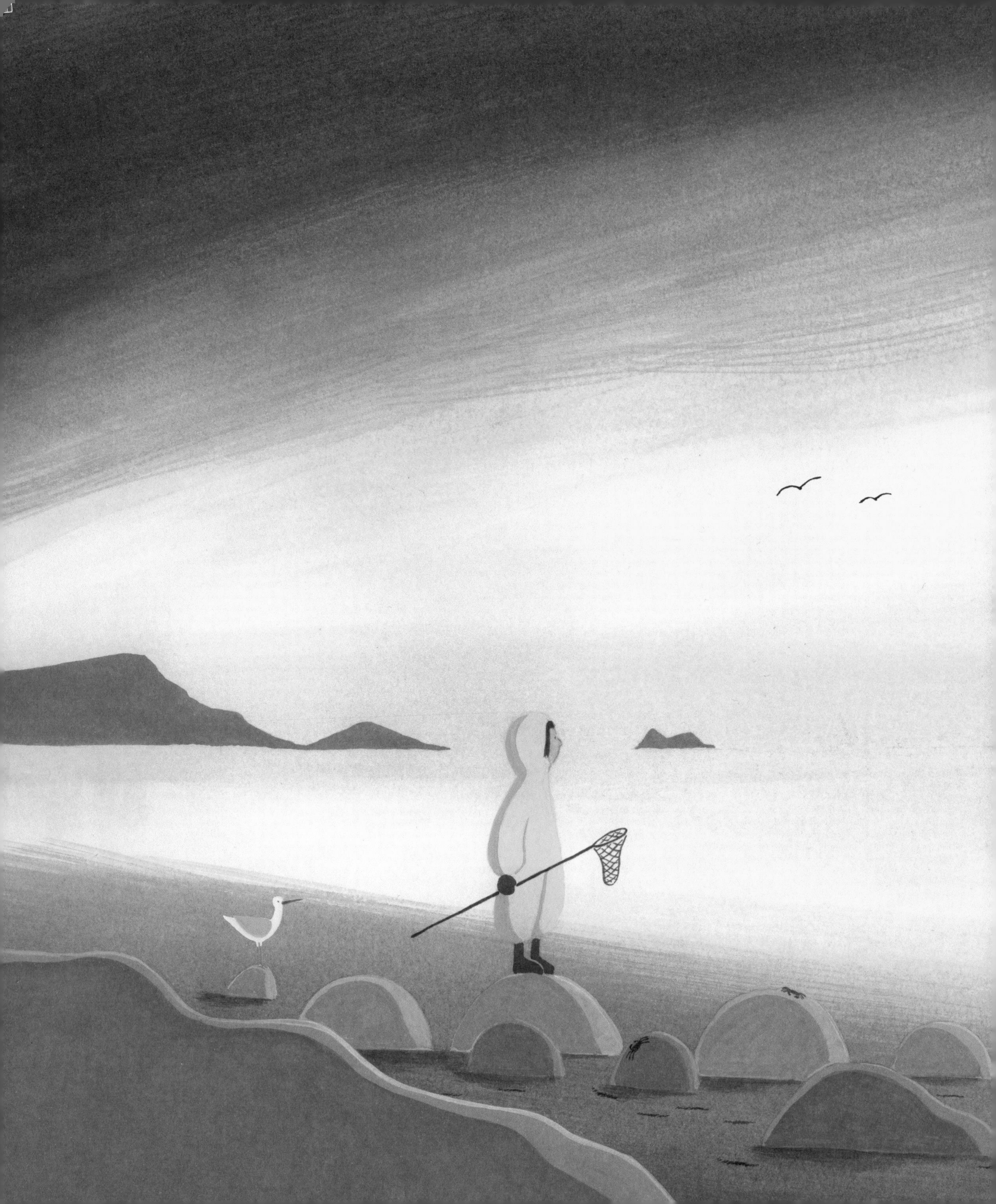

Cuno thought about these words endlessly.
For days, he watched, and watched,
and ignored little Aia who wanted to play.

"Have you seen it yet?"
she asked each afternoon.

"No, and stop distracting me. I search alone,"
was his reply.

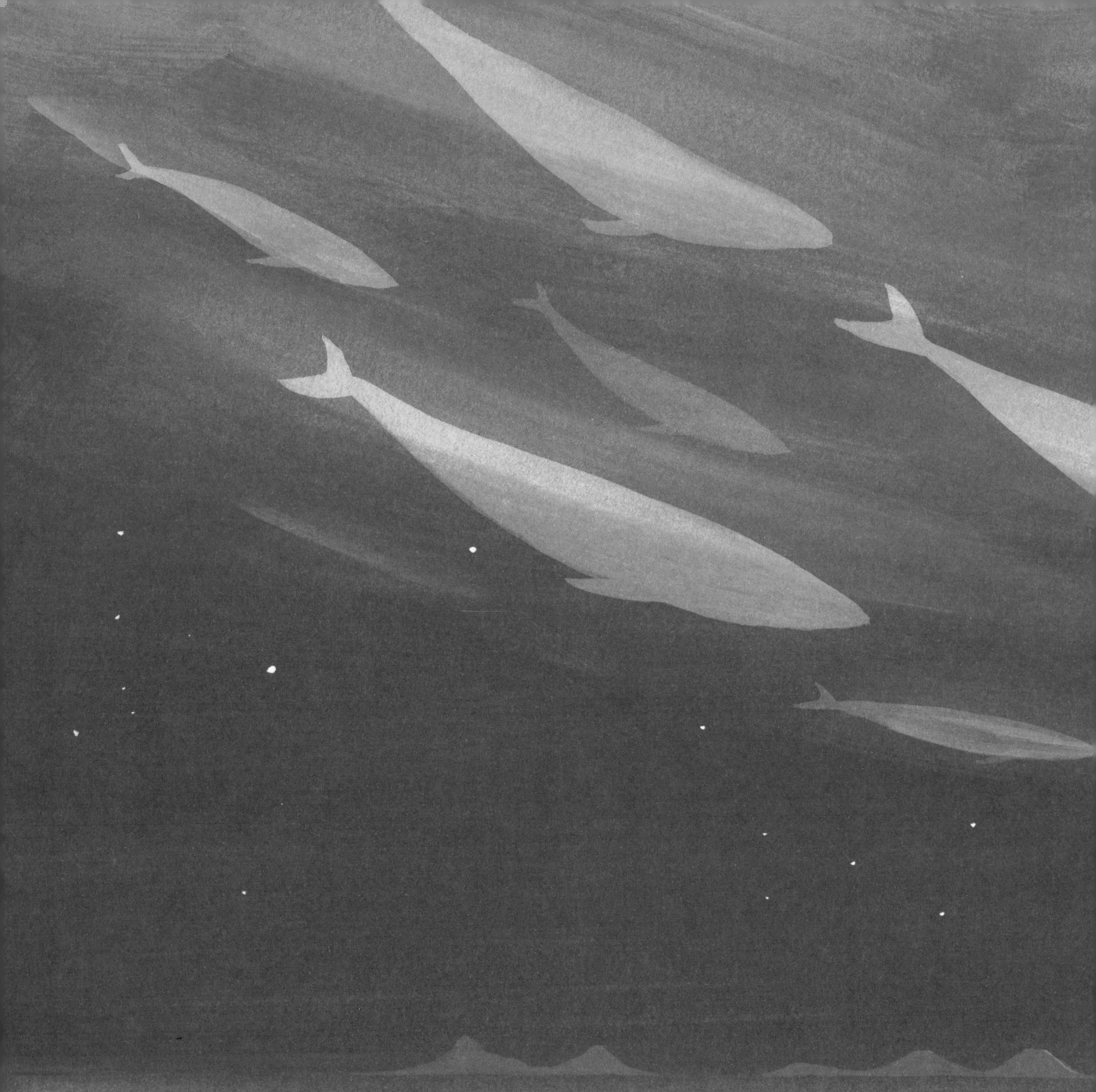

In the night, Cuno dreamed about the big beast. It drifted through the sea and made sounds that thundered throughout the land.

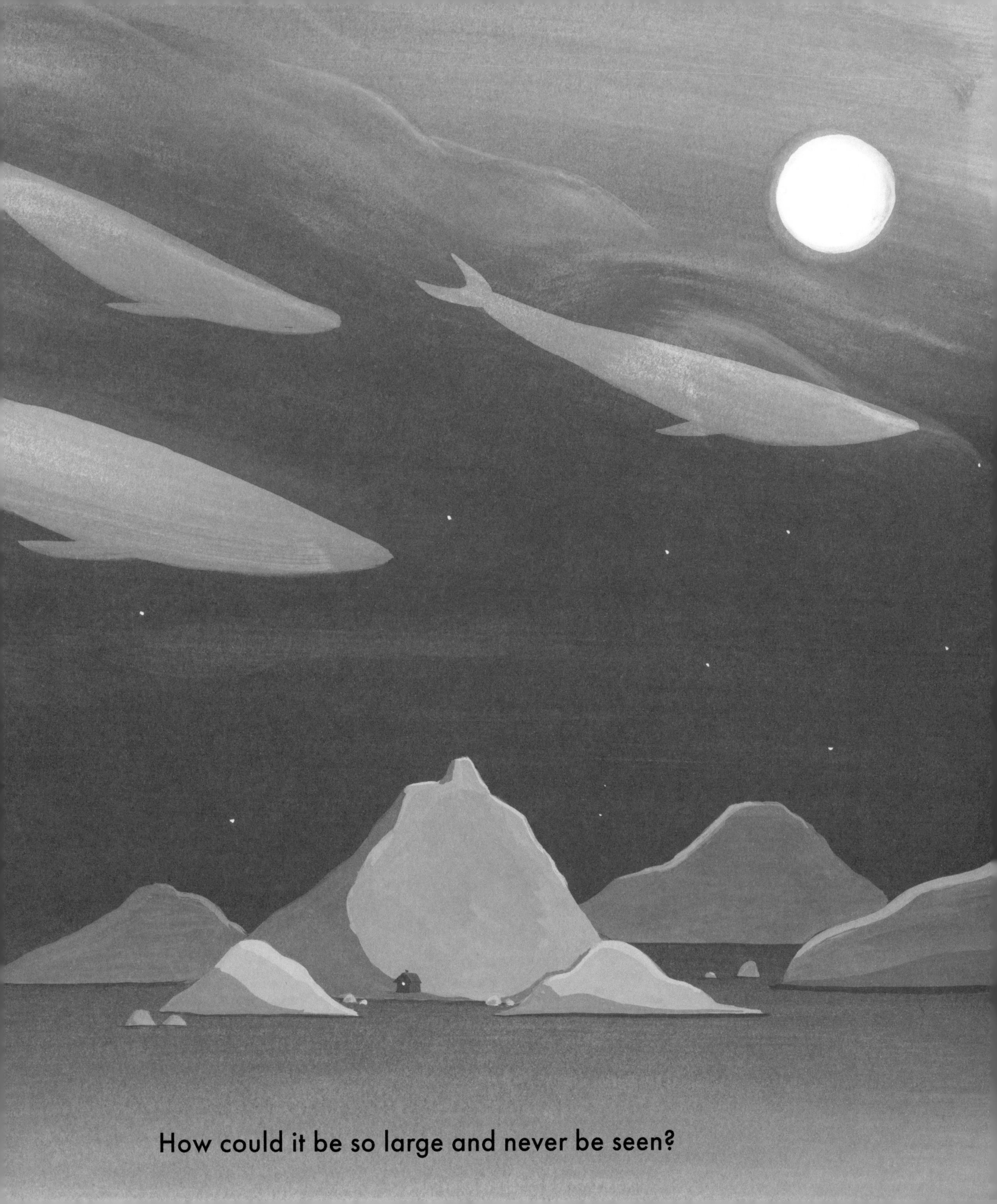

How could it be so large and never be seen?

One twinkling morning Cuno awoke.
He quietly left the house, took his father's
kayak, and crept into the bay.

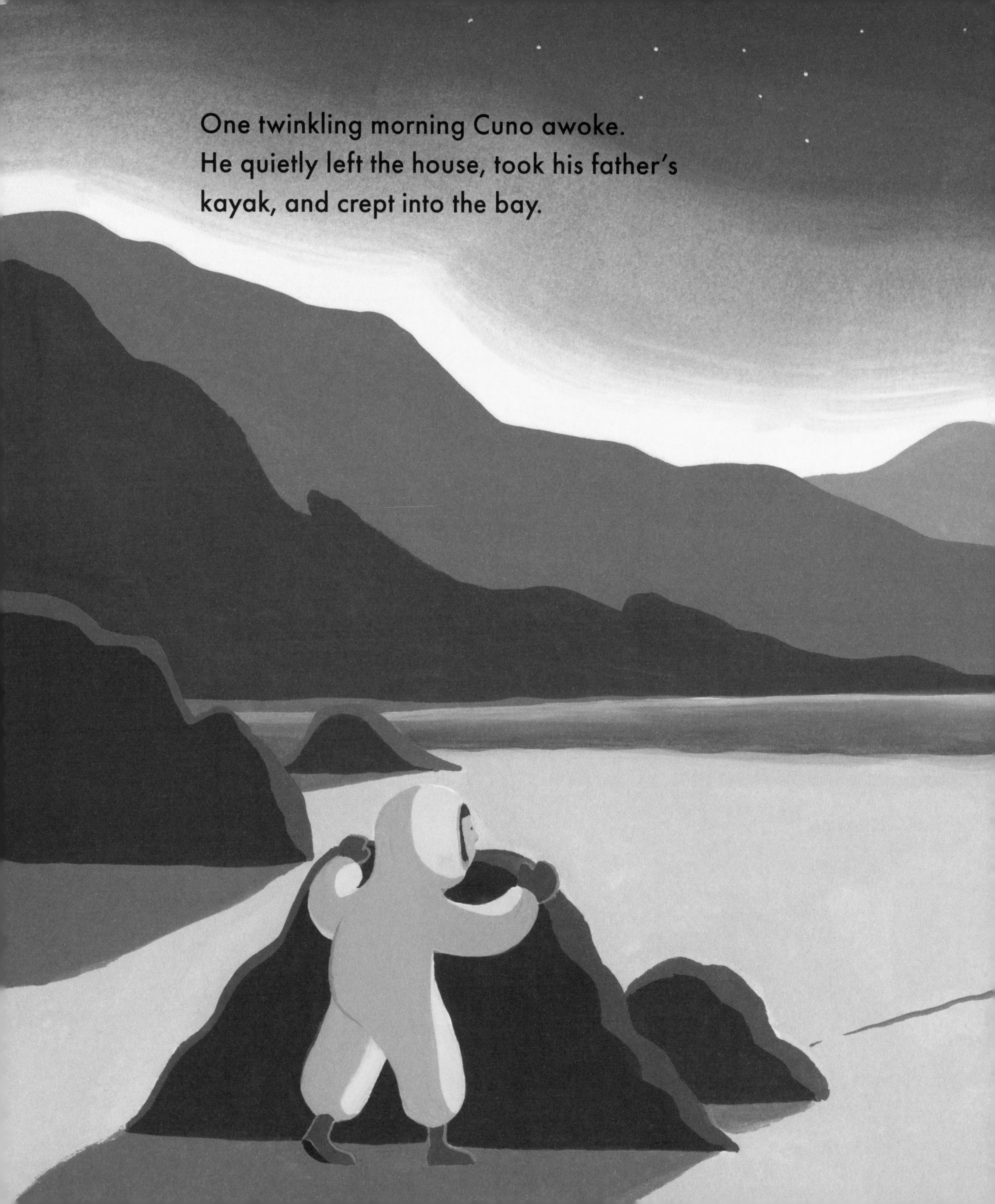

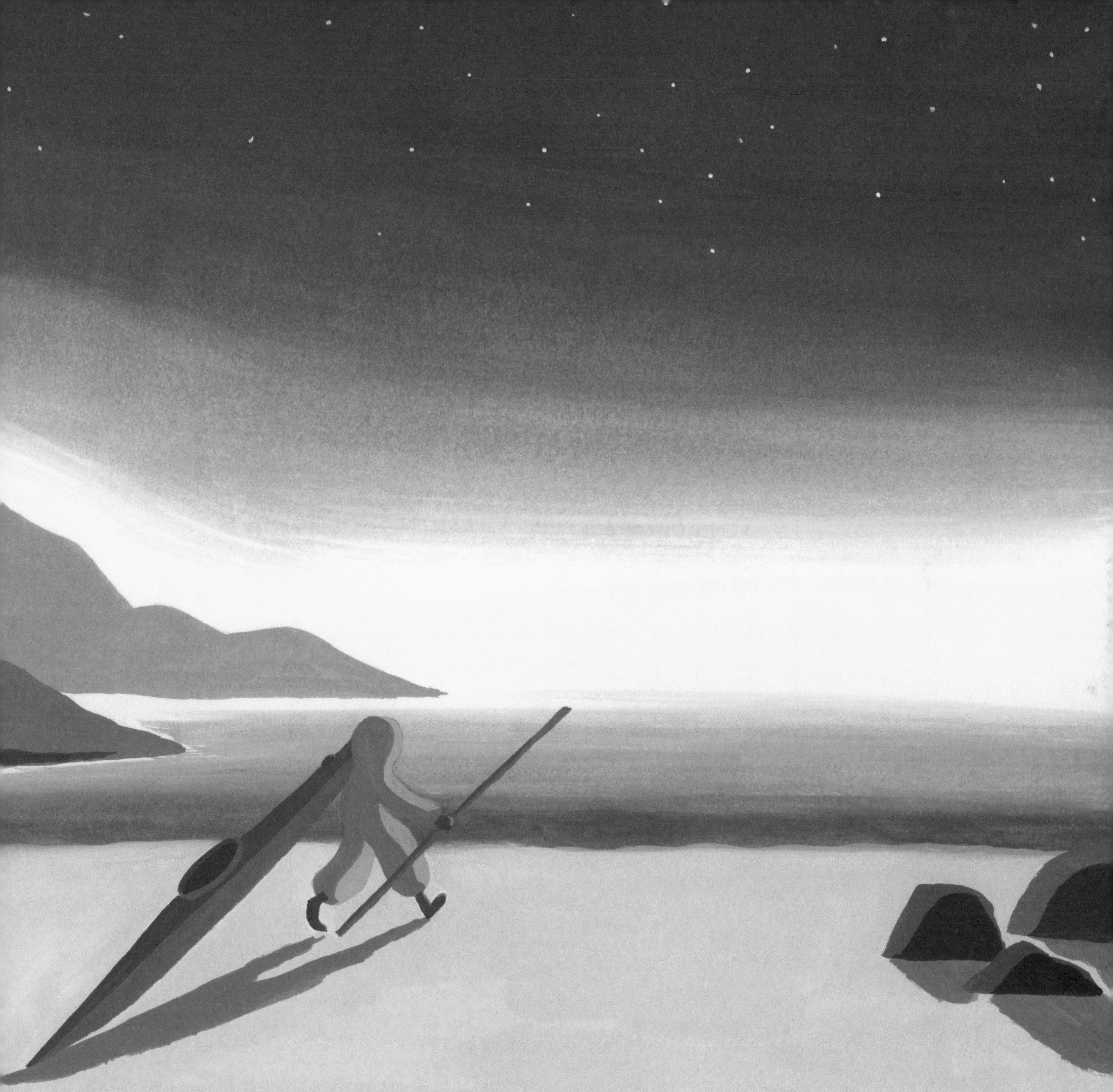

He would find the whale on his own.
Or so he thought.

The sea was very quiet, the gulls
swooped and glided above.

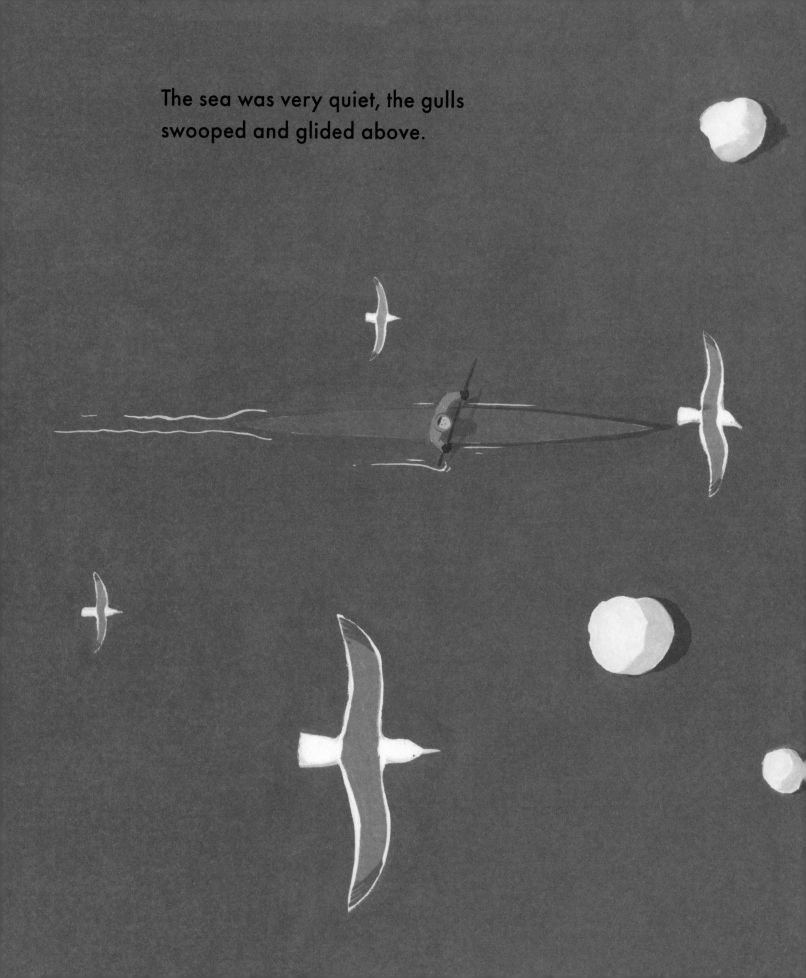

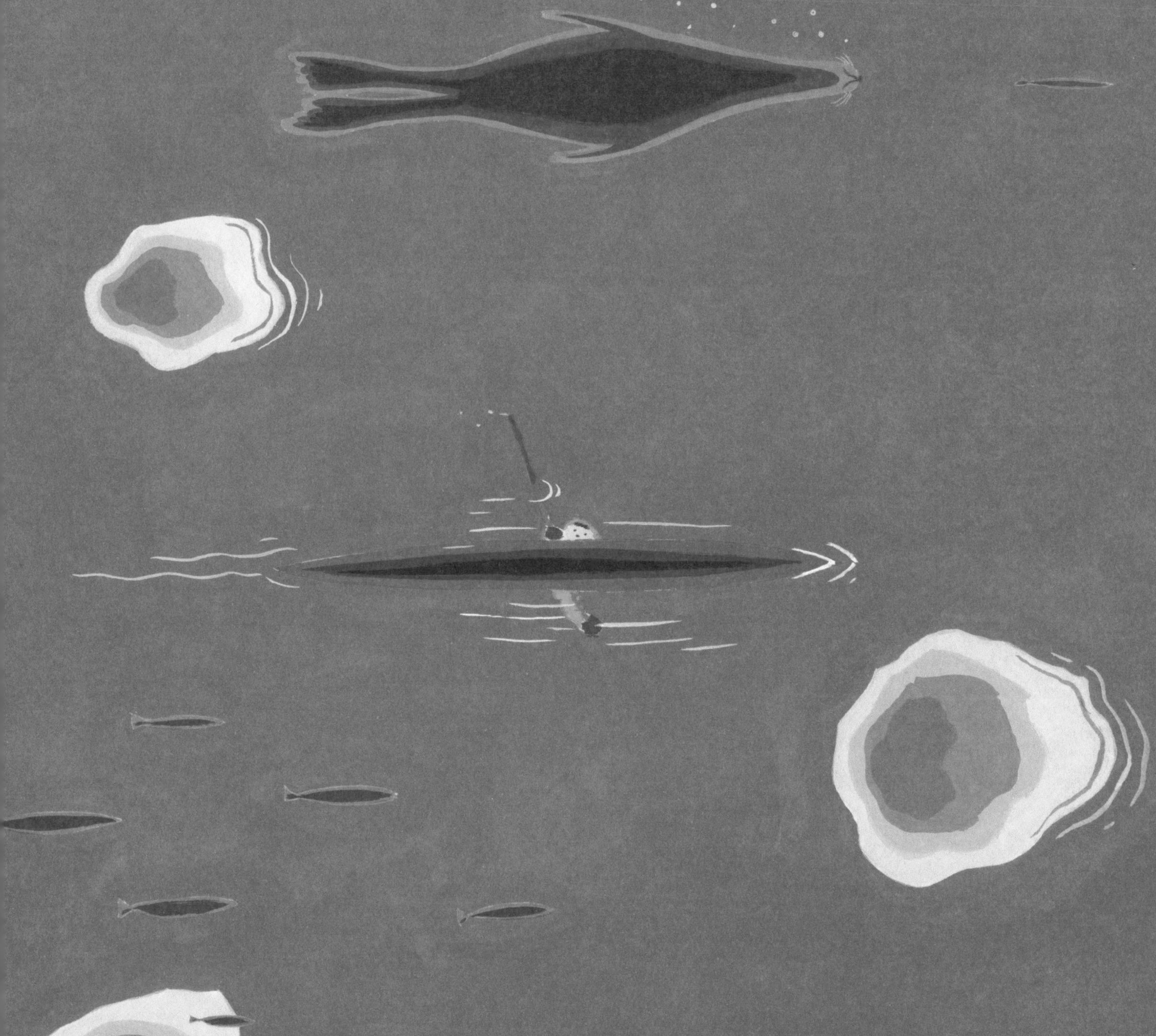

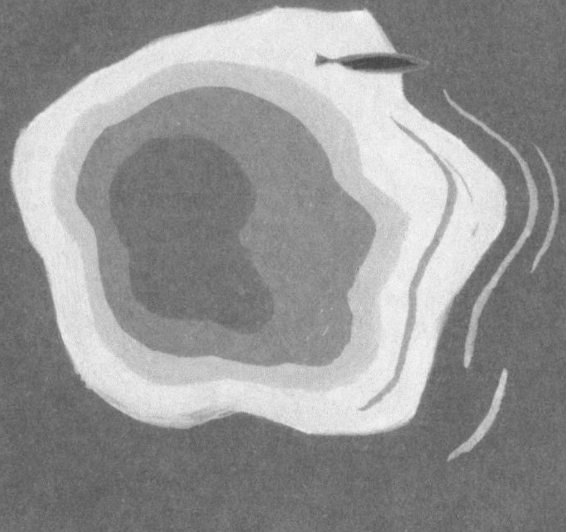

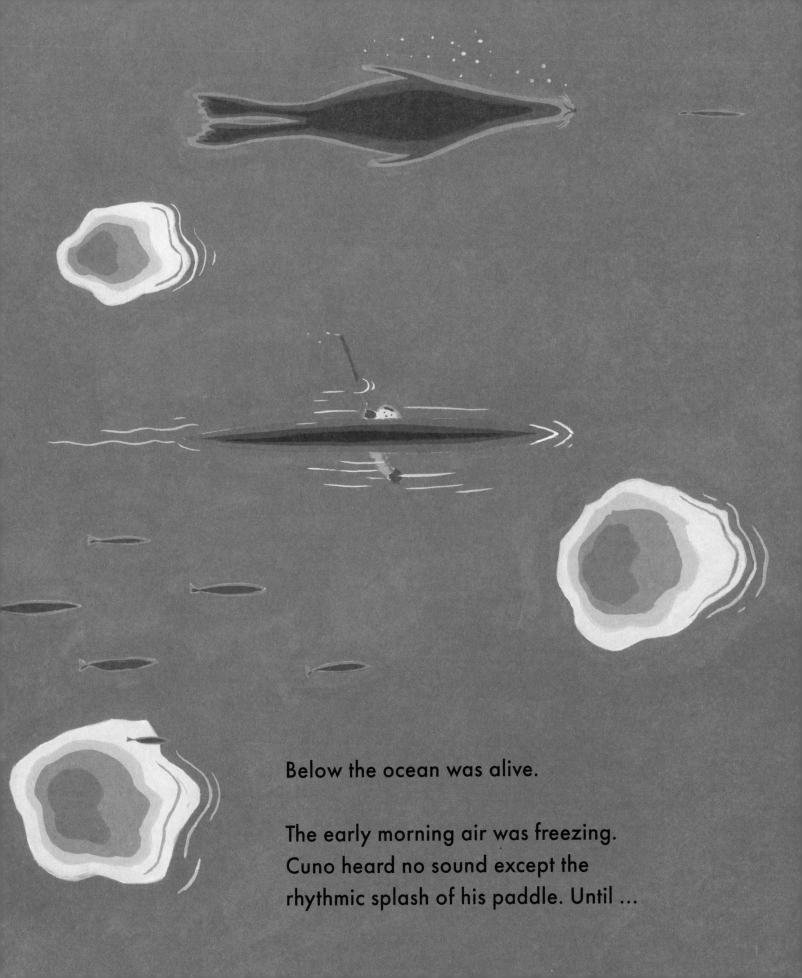

Below the ocean was alive.

The early morning air was freezing. Cuno heard no sound except the rhythmic splash of his paddle. Until ...

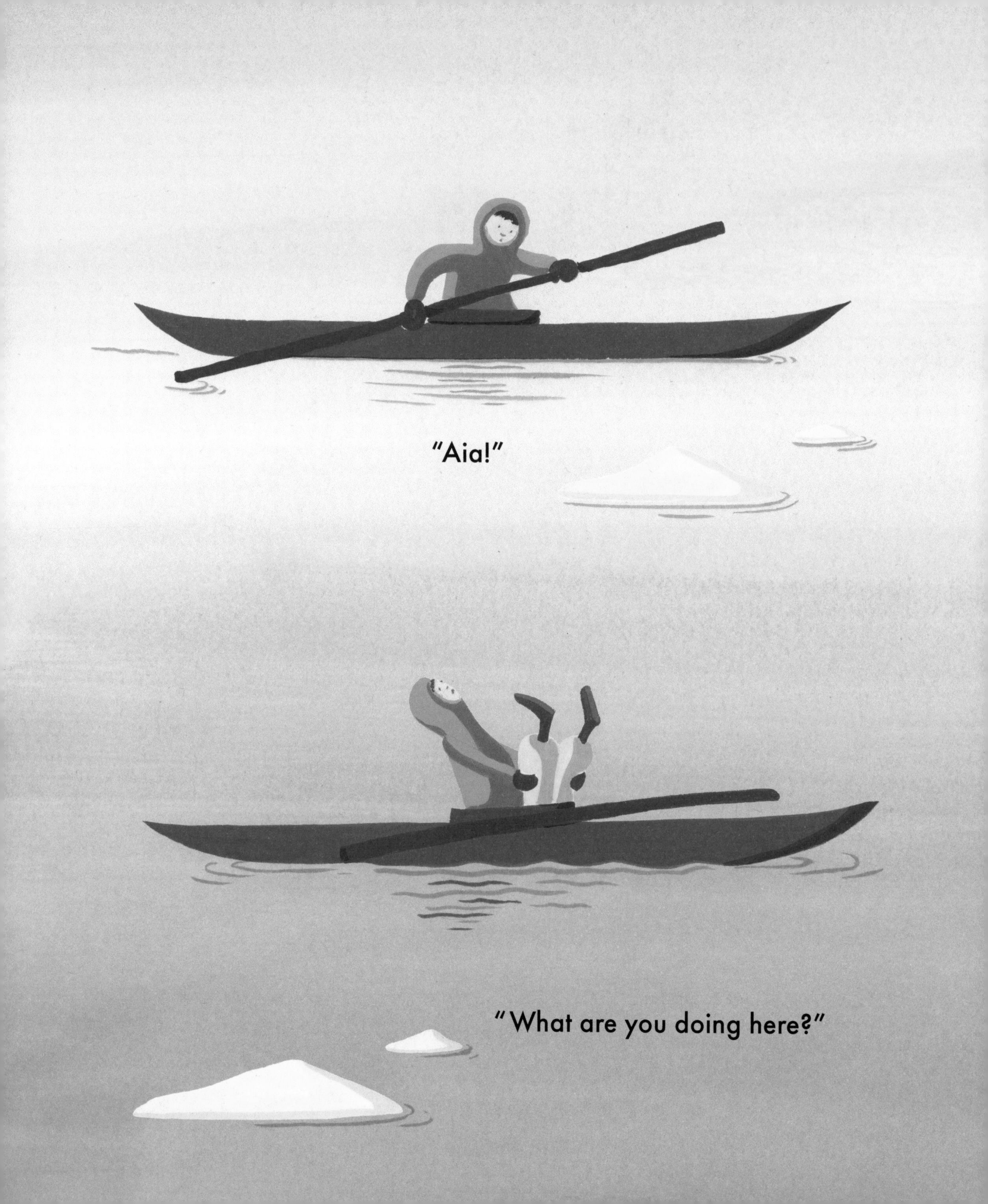
"Aia!"
"What are you doing here?"

"I want to help," she hooted with a grin.

Cuno was not at all pleased.
He put her in the back
and told her to keep quiet.

"Is that it there?" Aia cried.
"No, it's a geyser. They're pipes in the ground that shoot out steam."
"Like the kettle at home?" Aia squeaked.
"Yeah, kind of," said Cuno as he slowly paddled off.

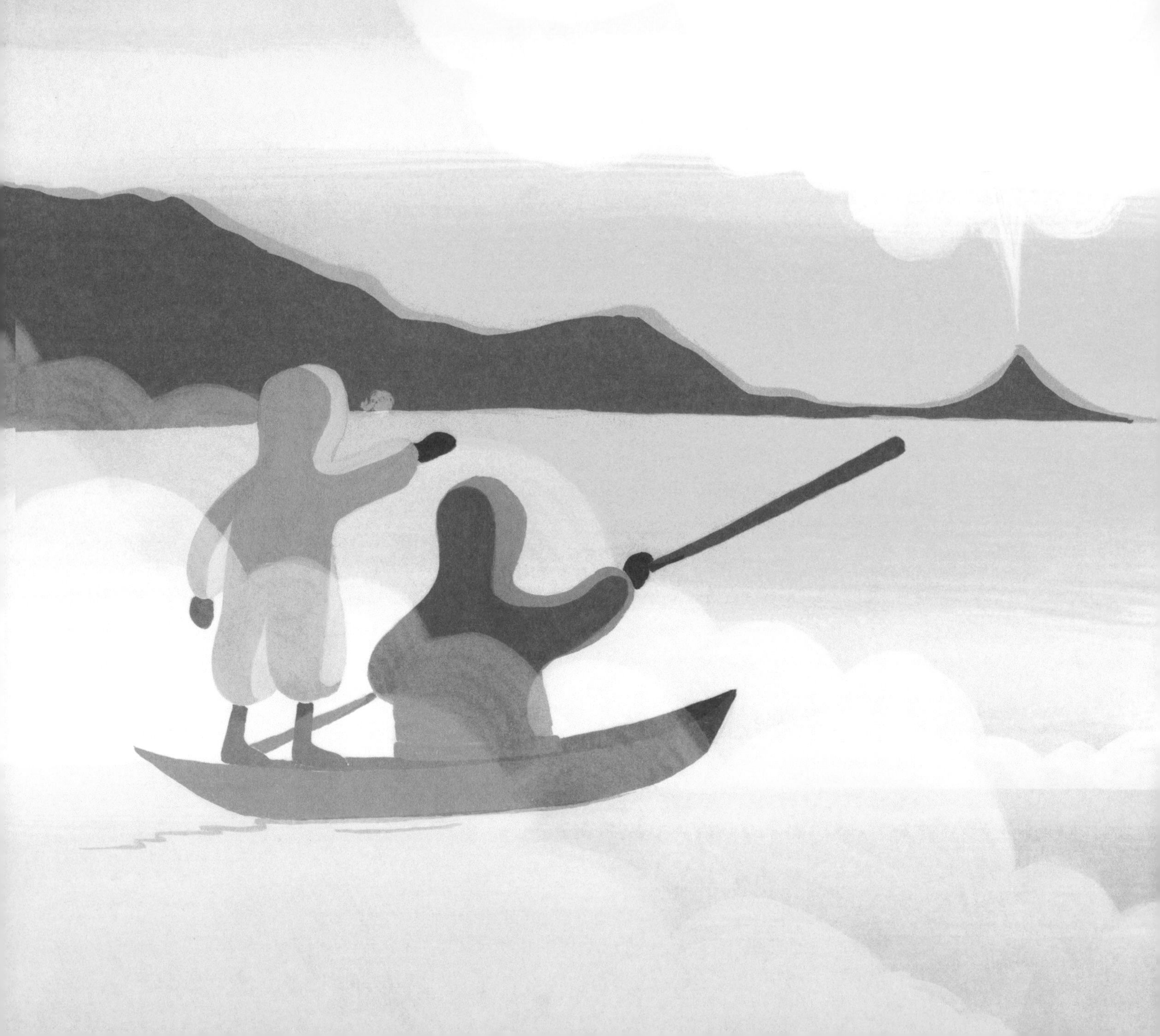

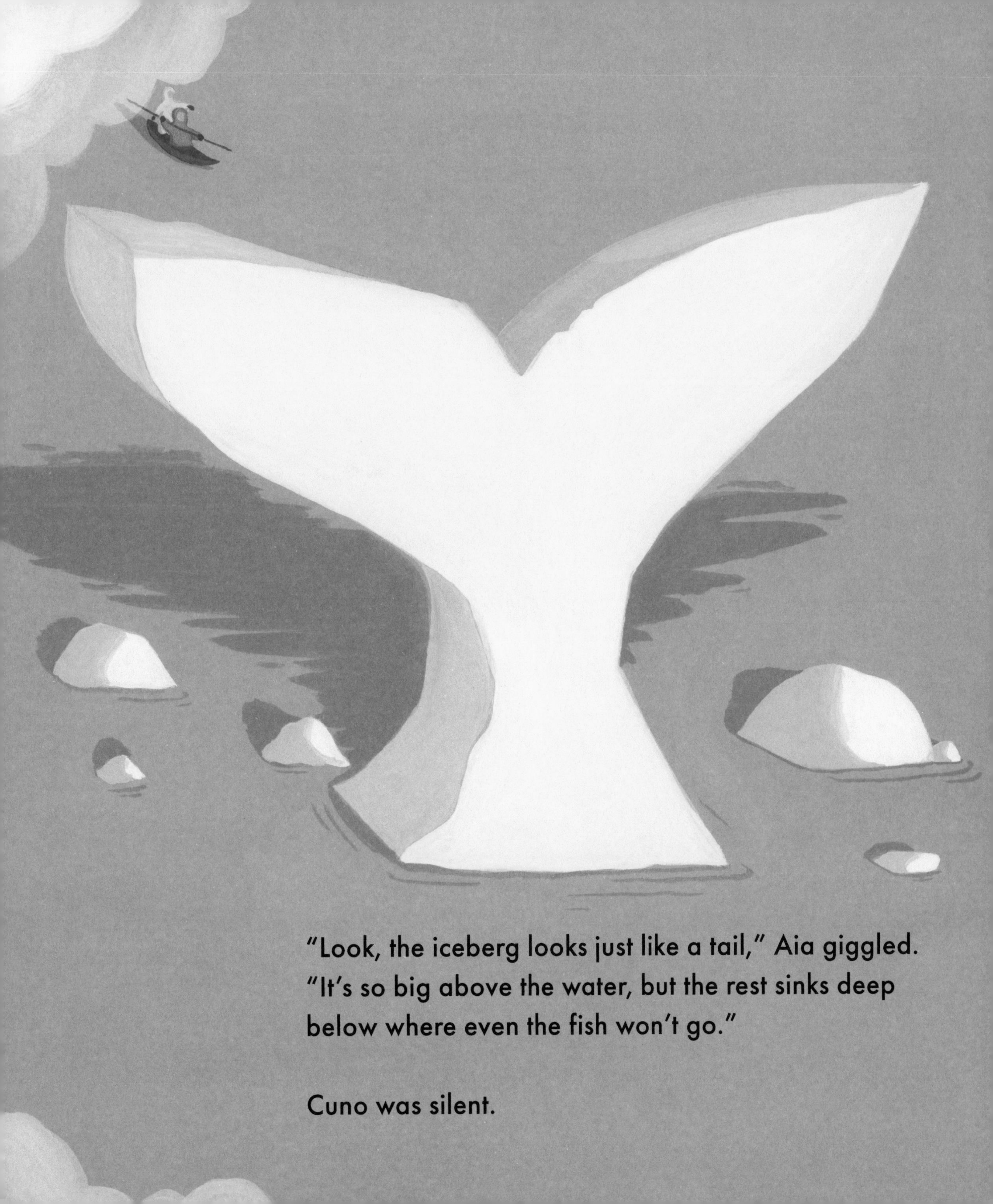

"Look, the iceberg looks just like a tail," Aia giggled. "It's so big above the water, but the rest sinks deep below where even the fish won't go."

Cuno was silent.

"Hello, hello," she shouted.
"Maybe it's hiding in there."

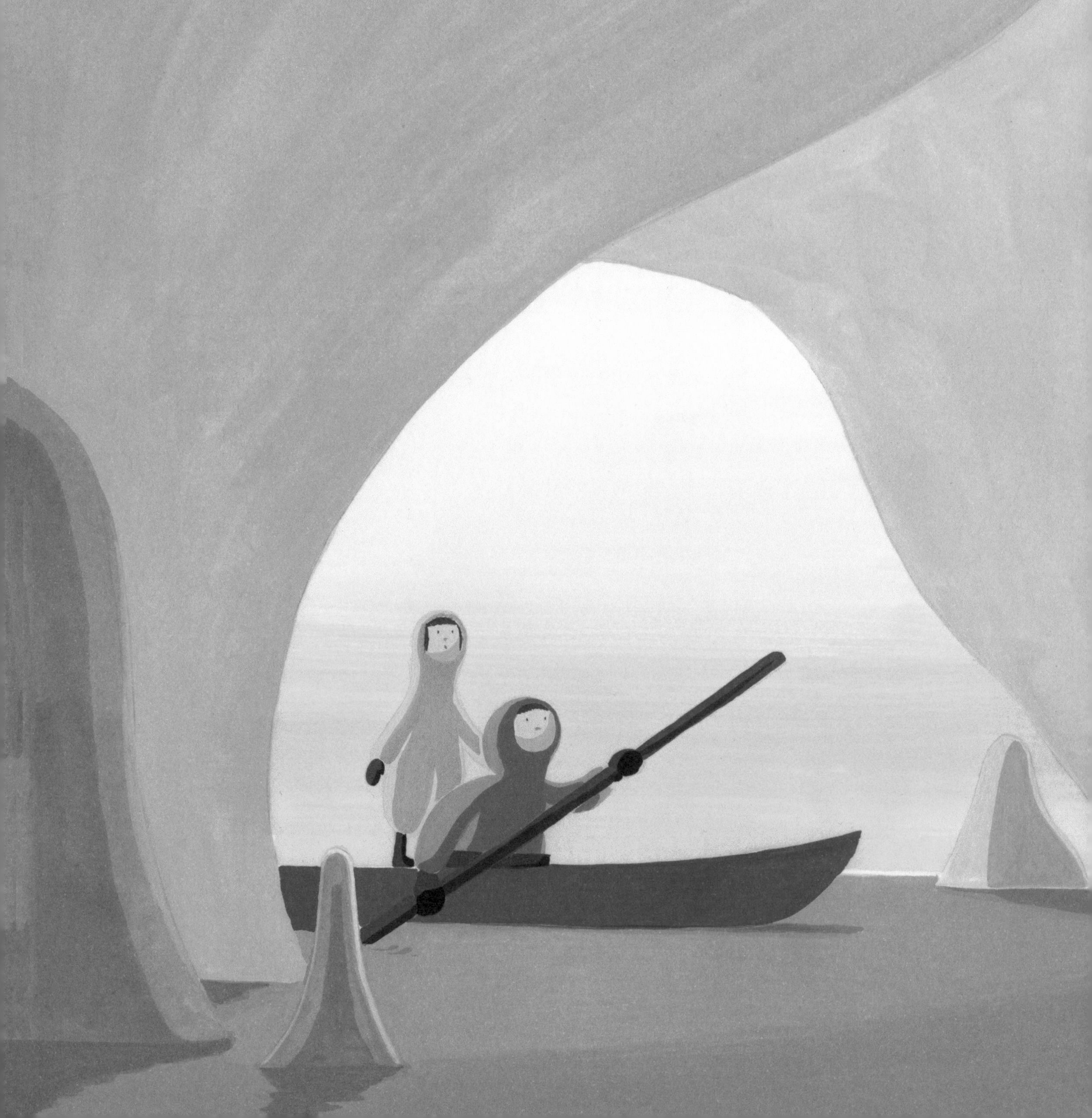

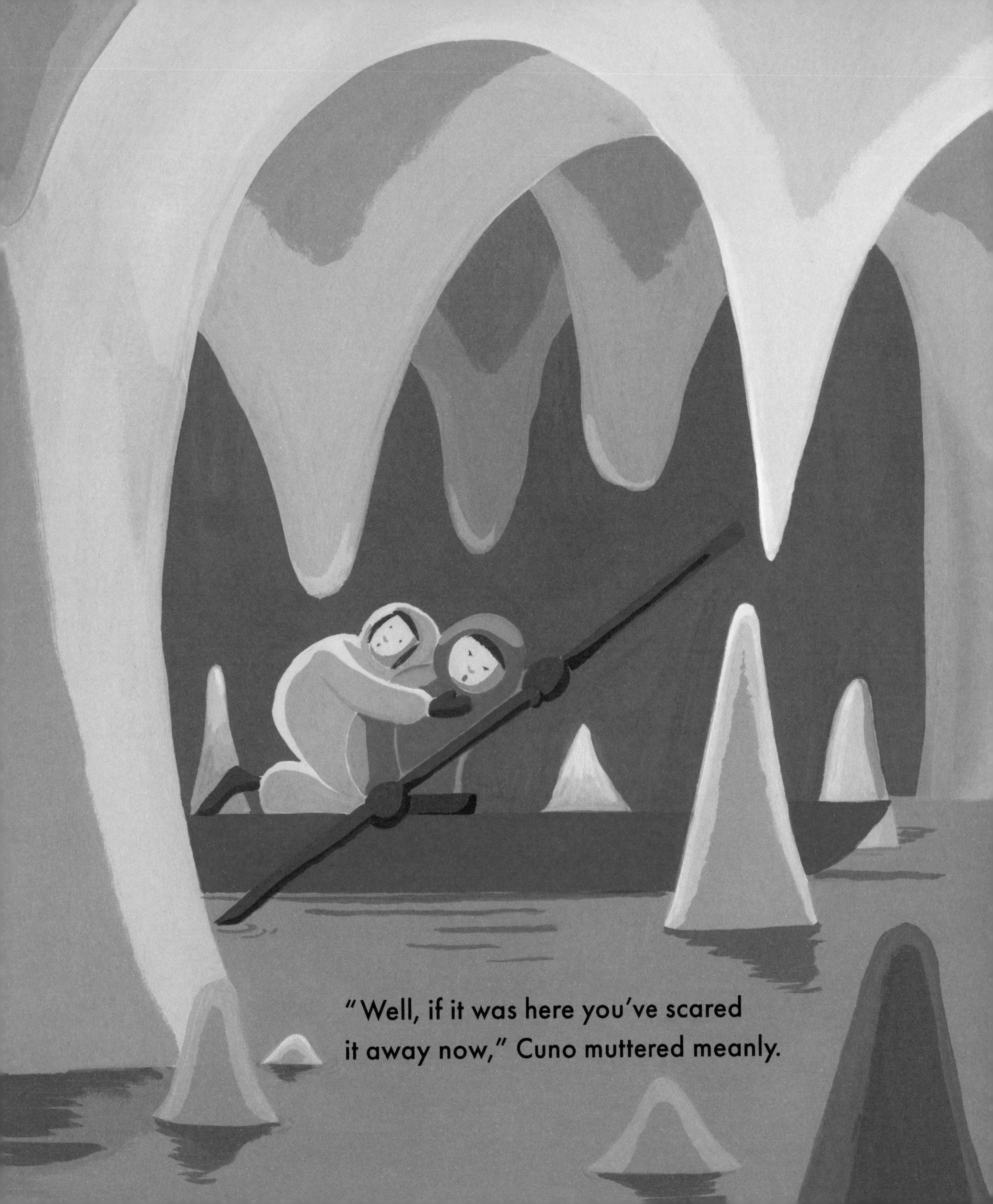

"Well, if it was here you've scared
it away now," Cuno muttered meanly.

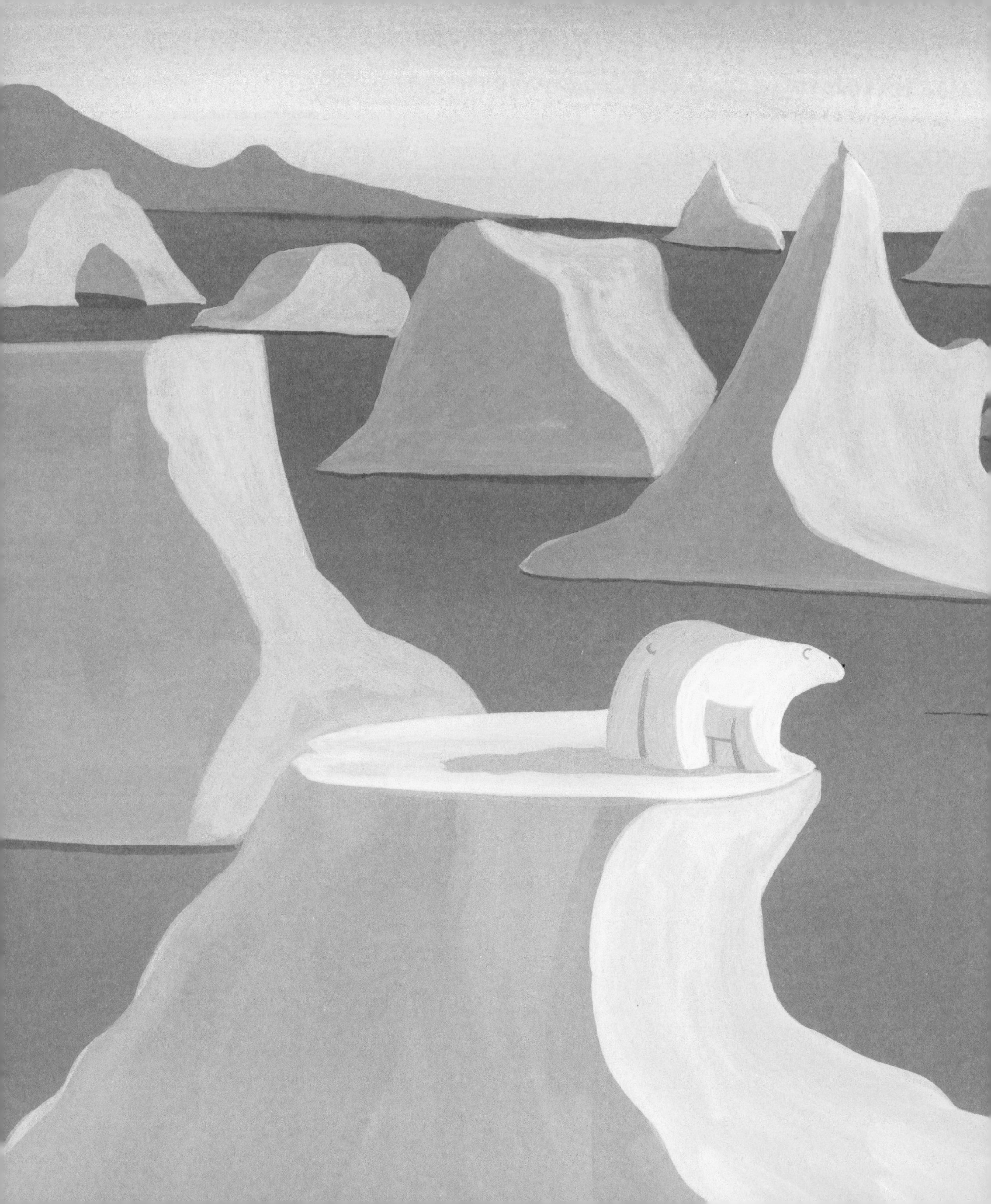

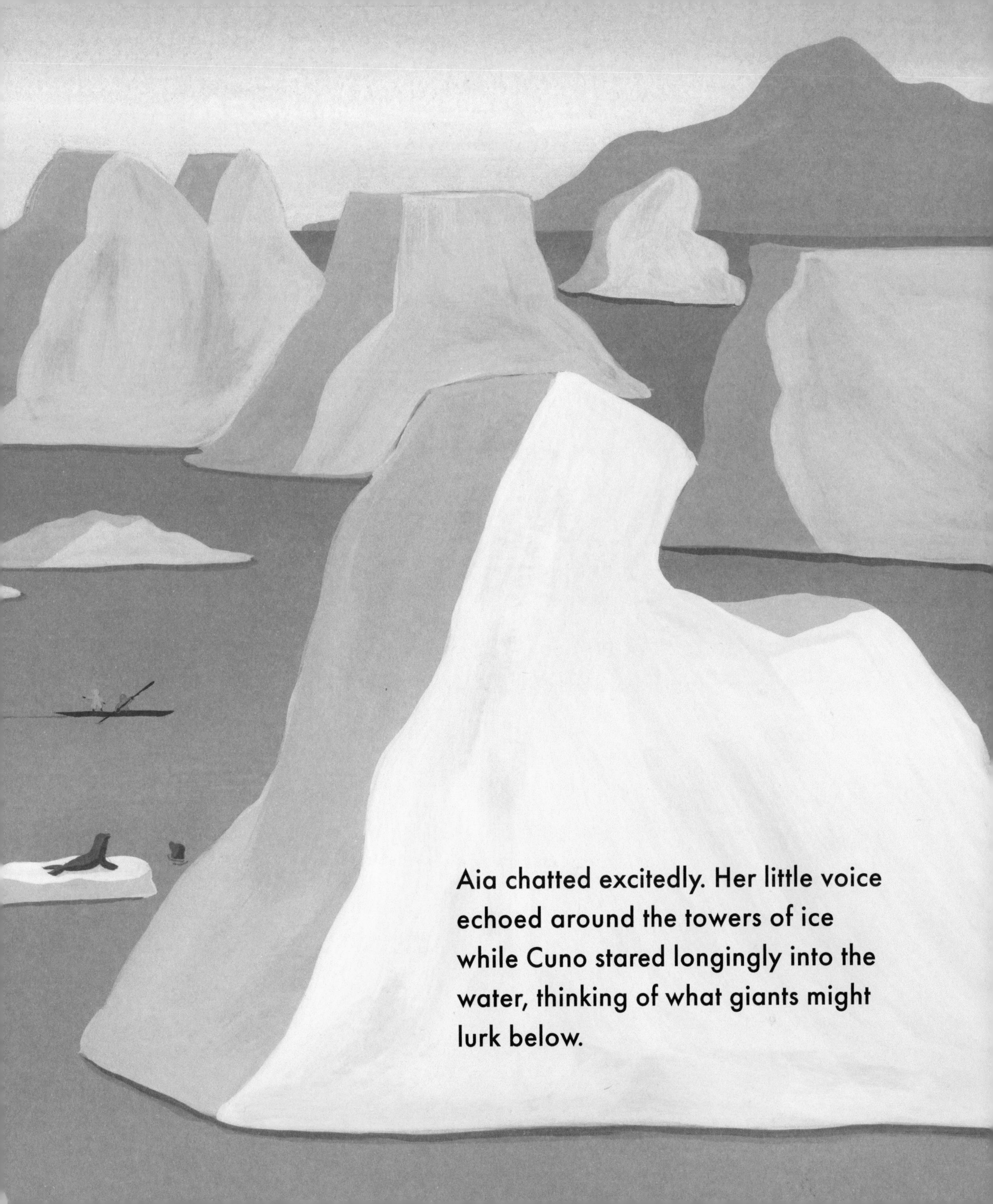

Aia chatted excitedly. Her little voice echoed around the towers of ice while Cuno stared longingly into the water, thinking of what giants might lurk below.

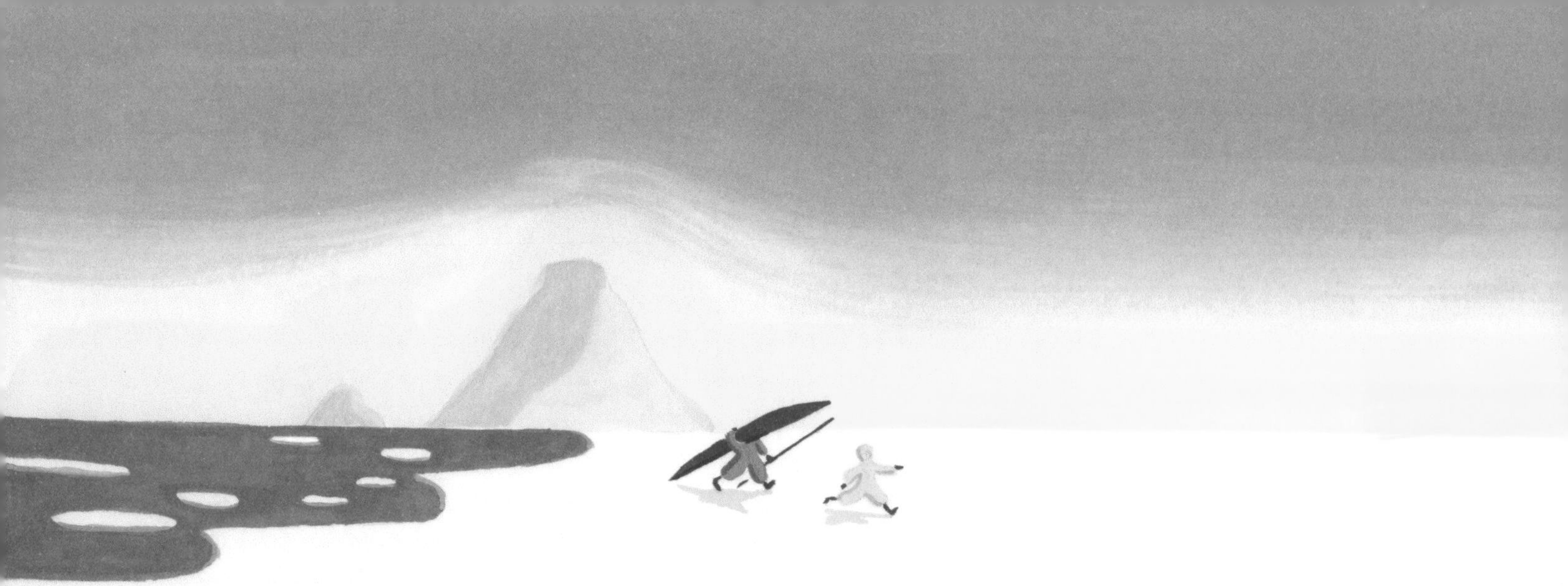

When the ice became too packed,
they took to the land.

"We're never going to find it now," Cuno huffed.

But Aia took no notice. "Look, ice bubbles!
Maybe they were made by an animal below."

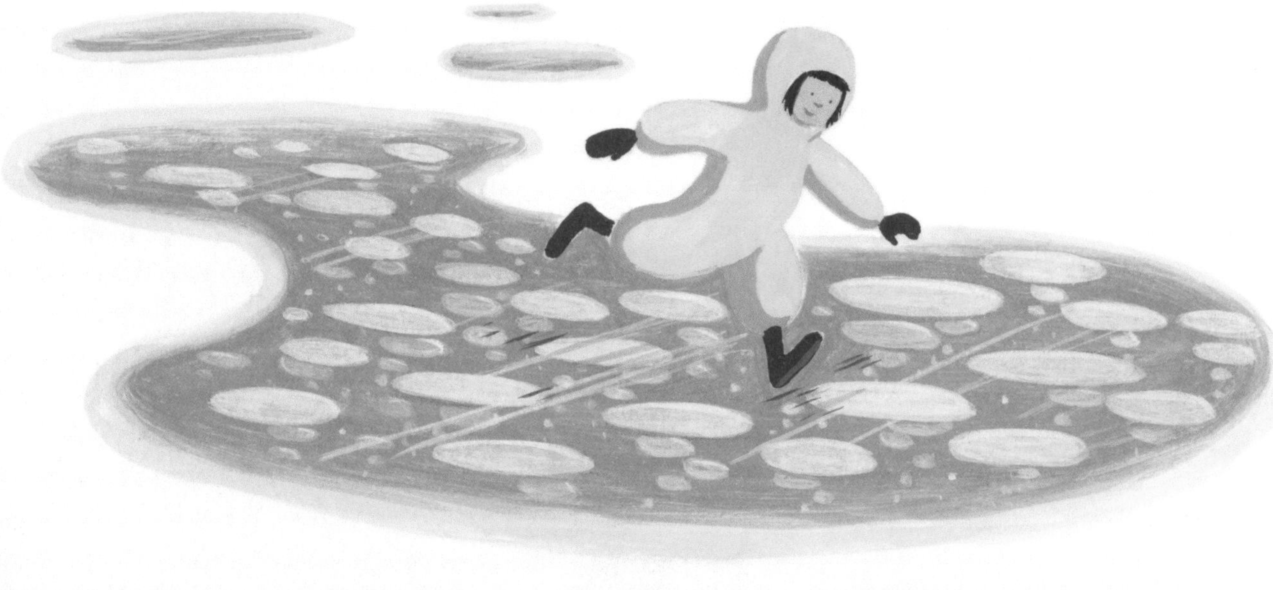

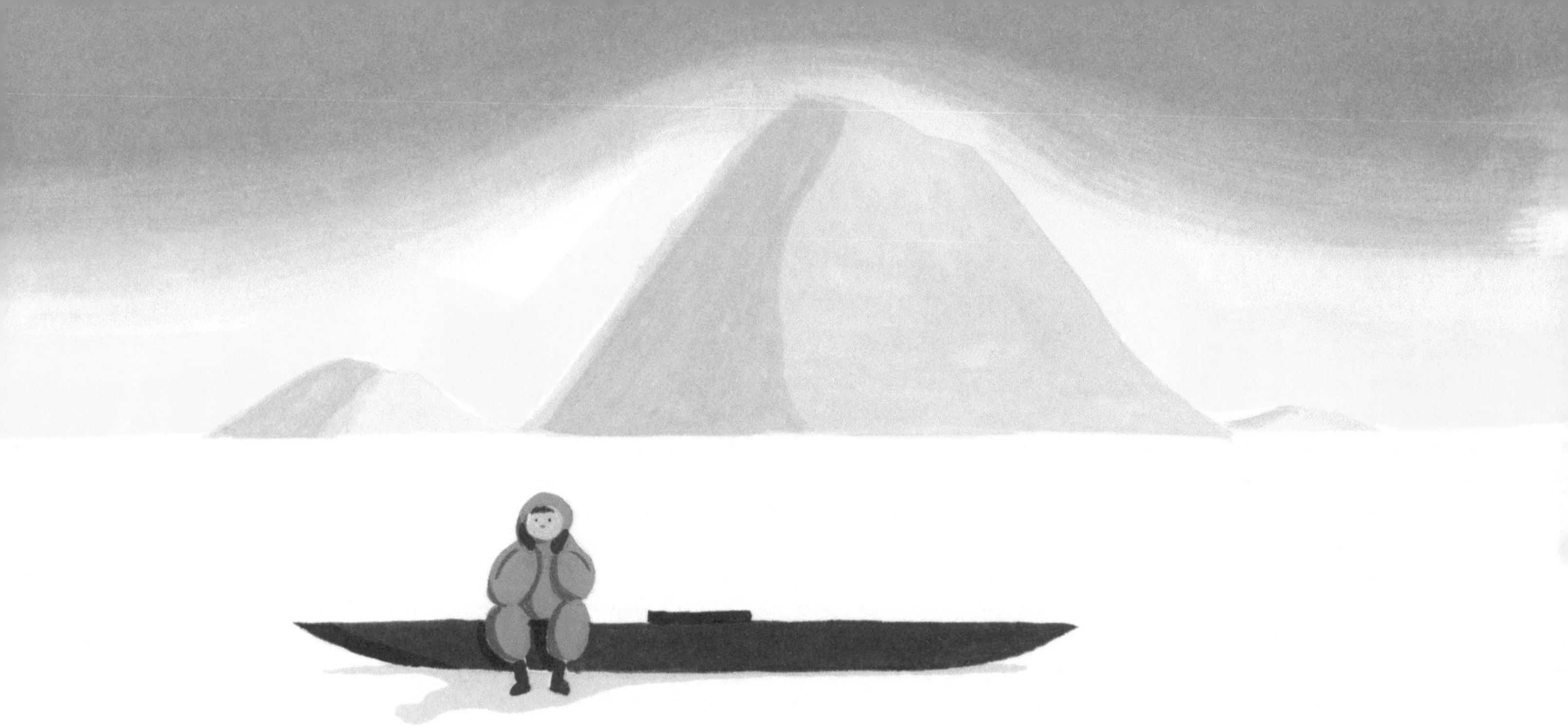

Cuno was getting more and more cross
as Aia clattered around.

"Stop it," he warned. "I'll leave you here
if you hurt yourself."

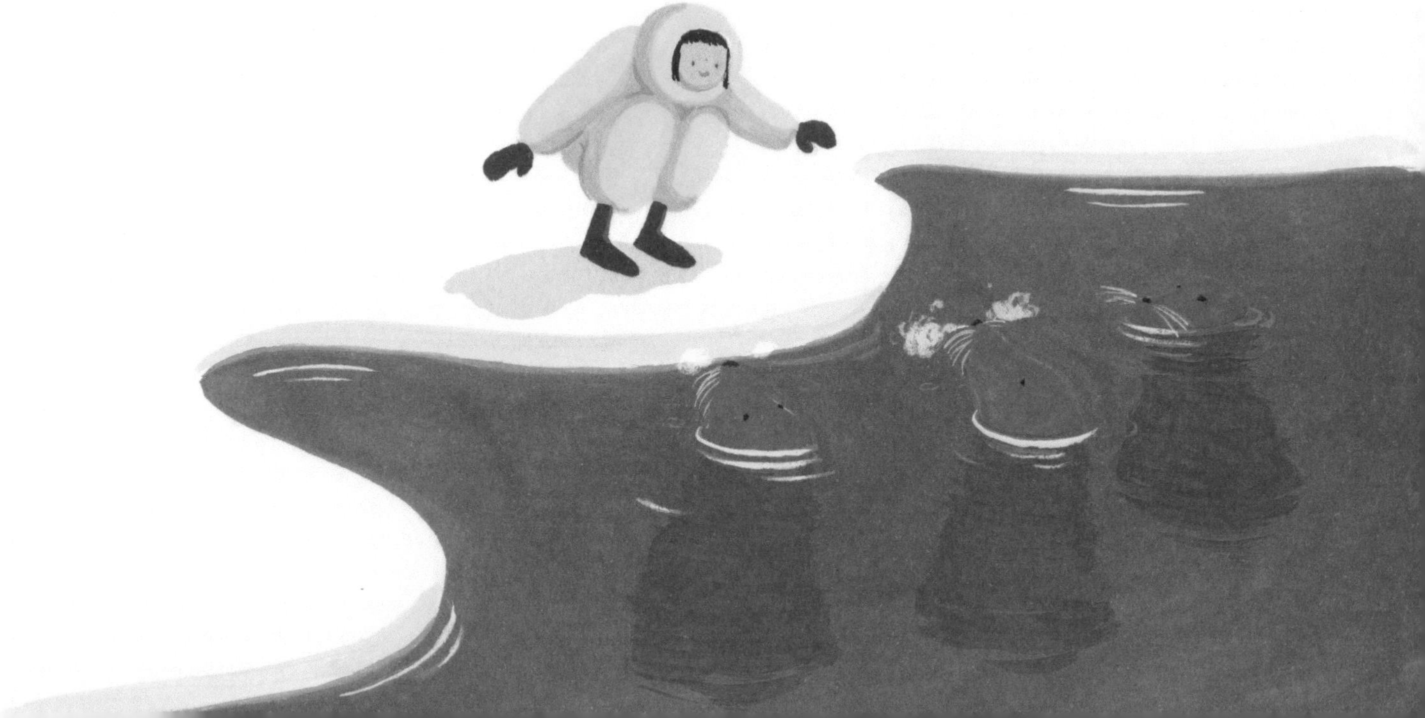

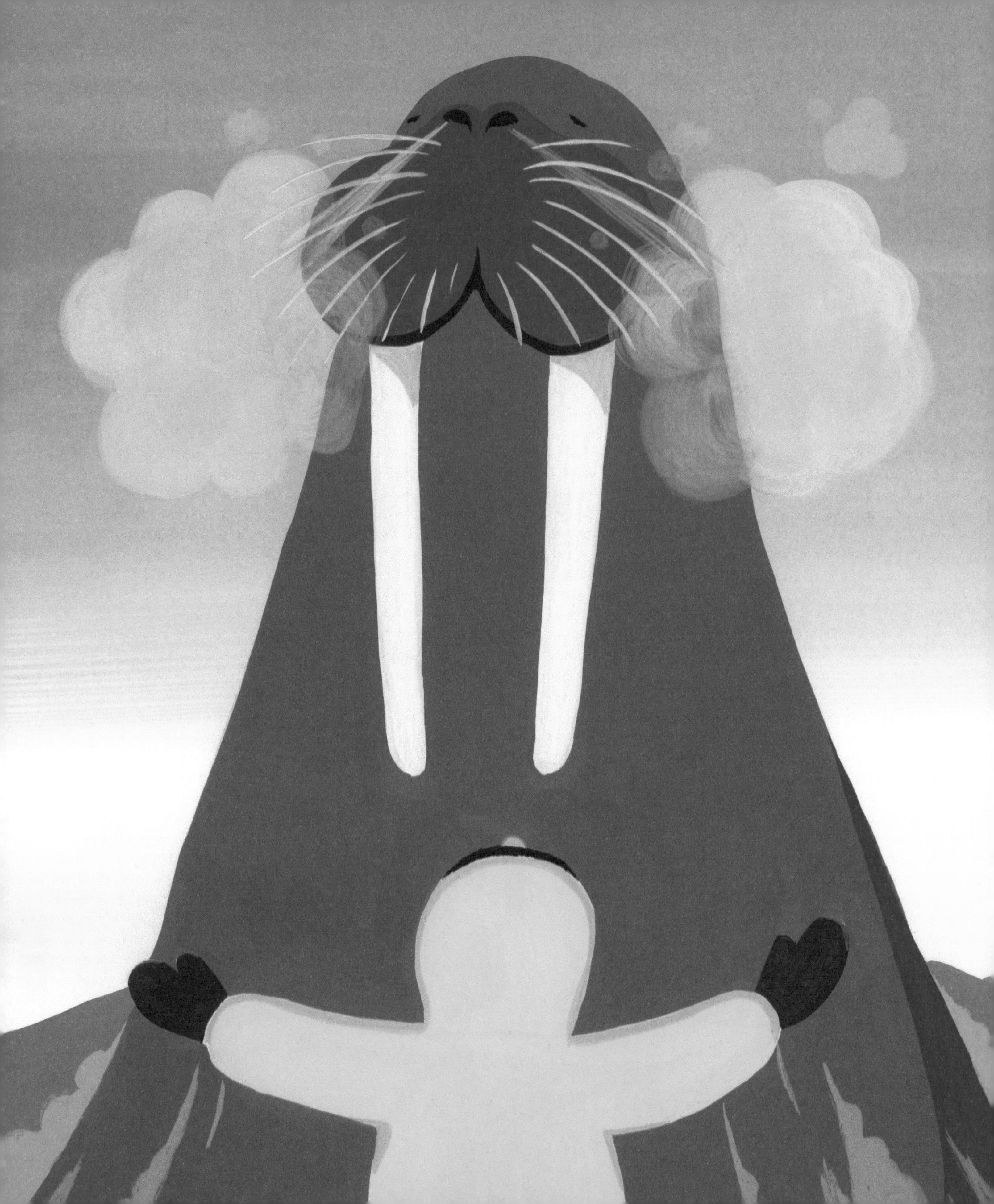

All this play was attracting unwanted attention.
And with a sudden crack, the ground shattered.
Aia screamed and slipped back. The ice broke away.

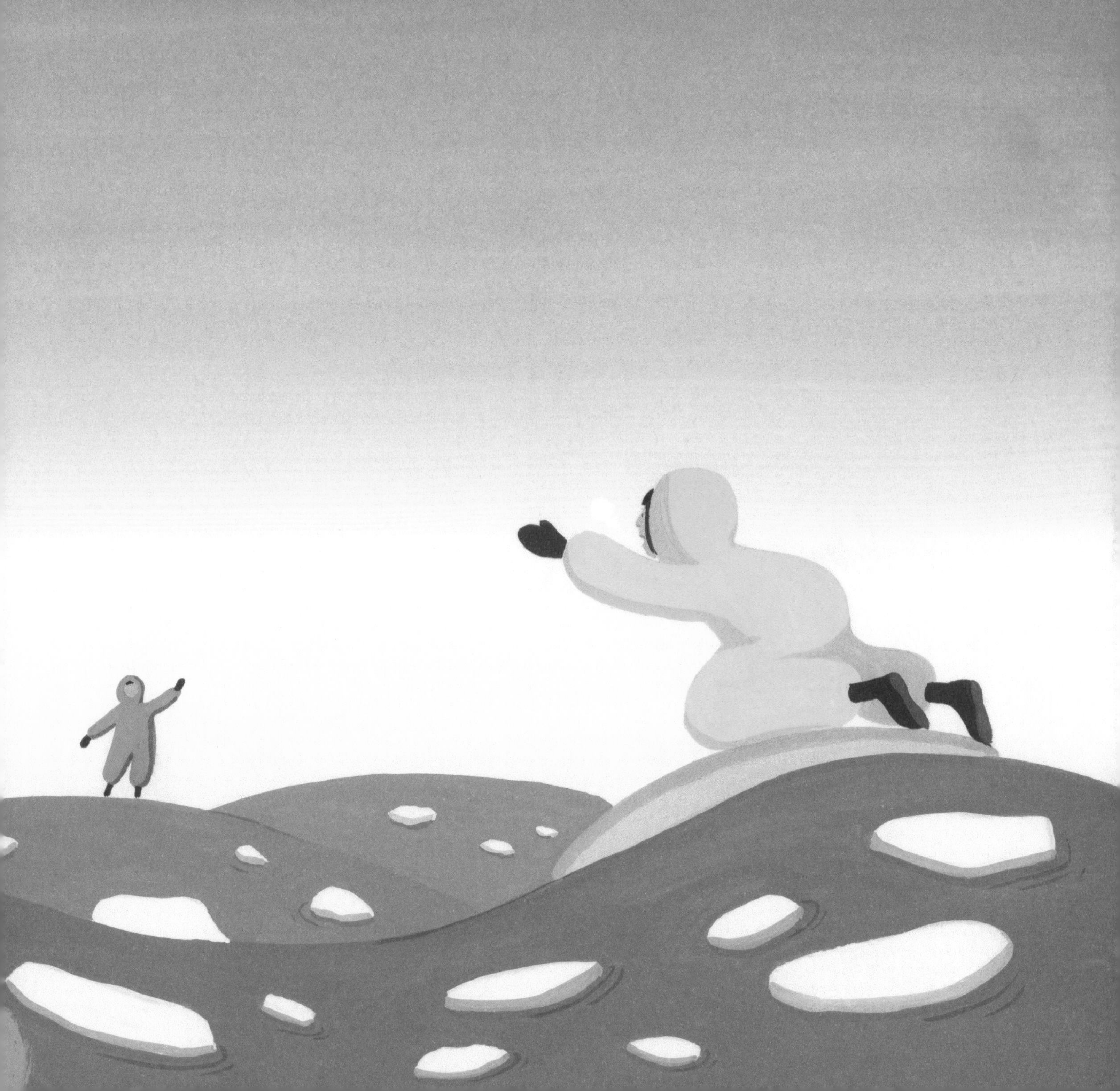

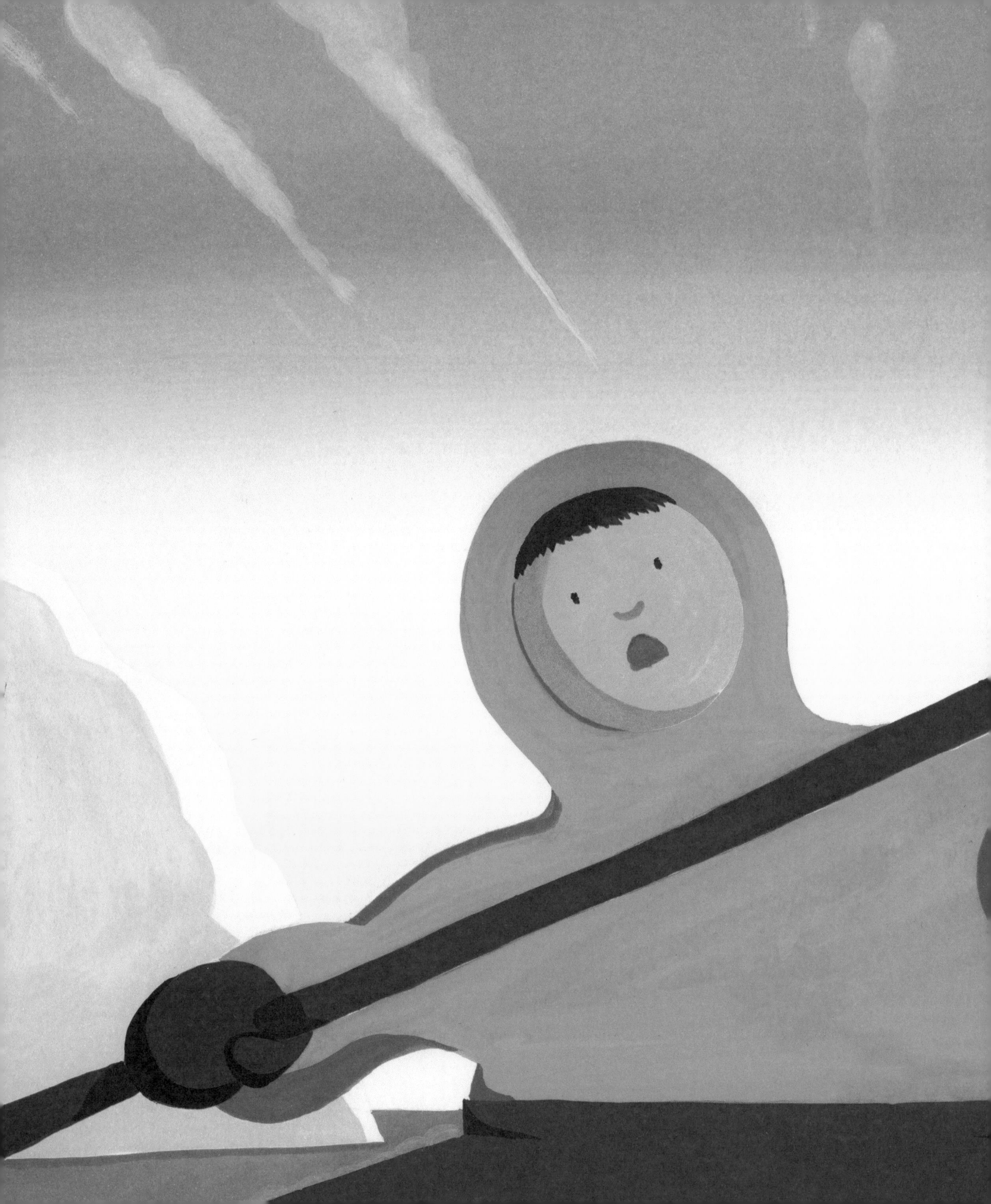

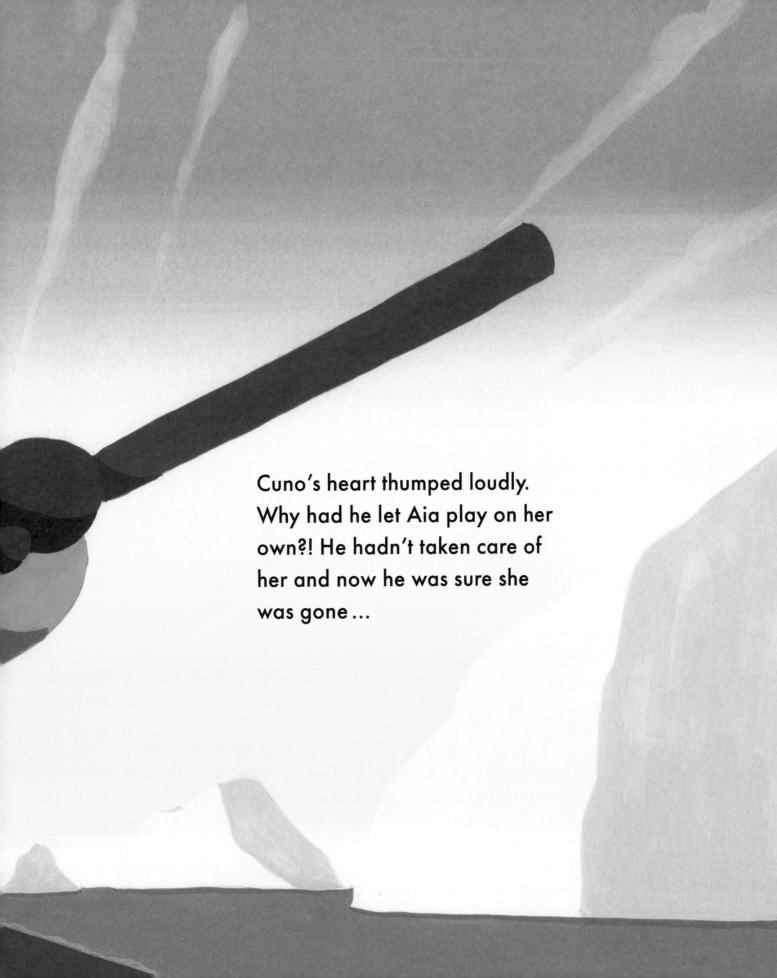

Cuno's heart thumped loudly. Why had he let Aia play on her own?! He hadn't taken care of her and now he was sure she was gone …

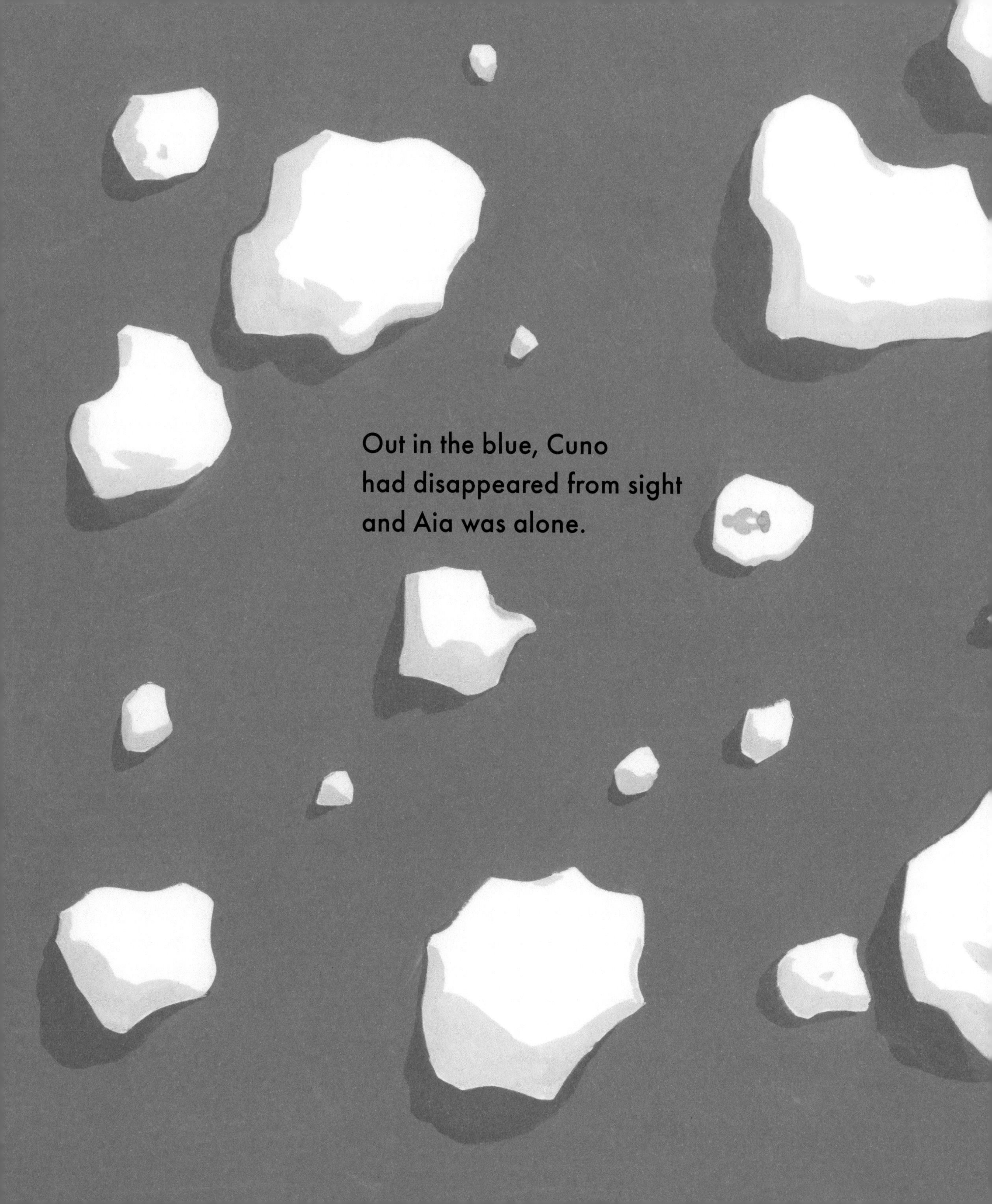

Out in the blue, Cuno
had disappeared from sight
and Aia was alone.

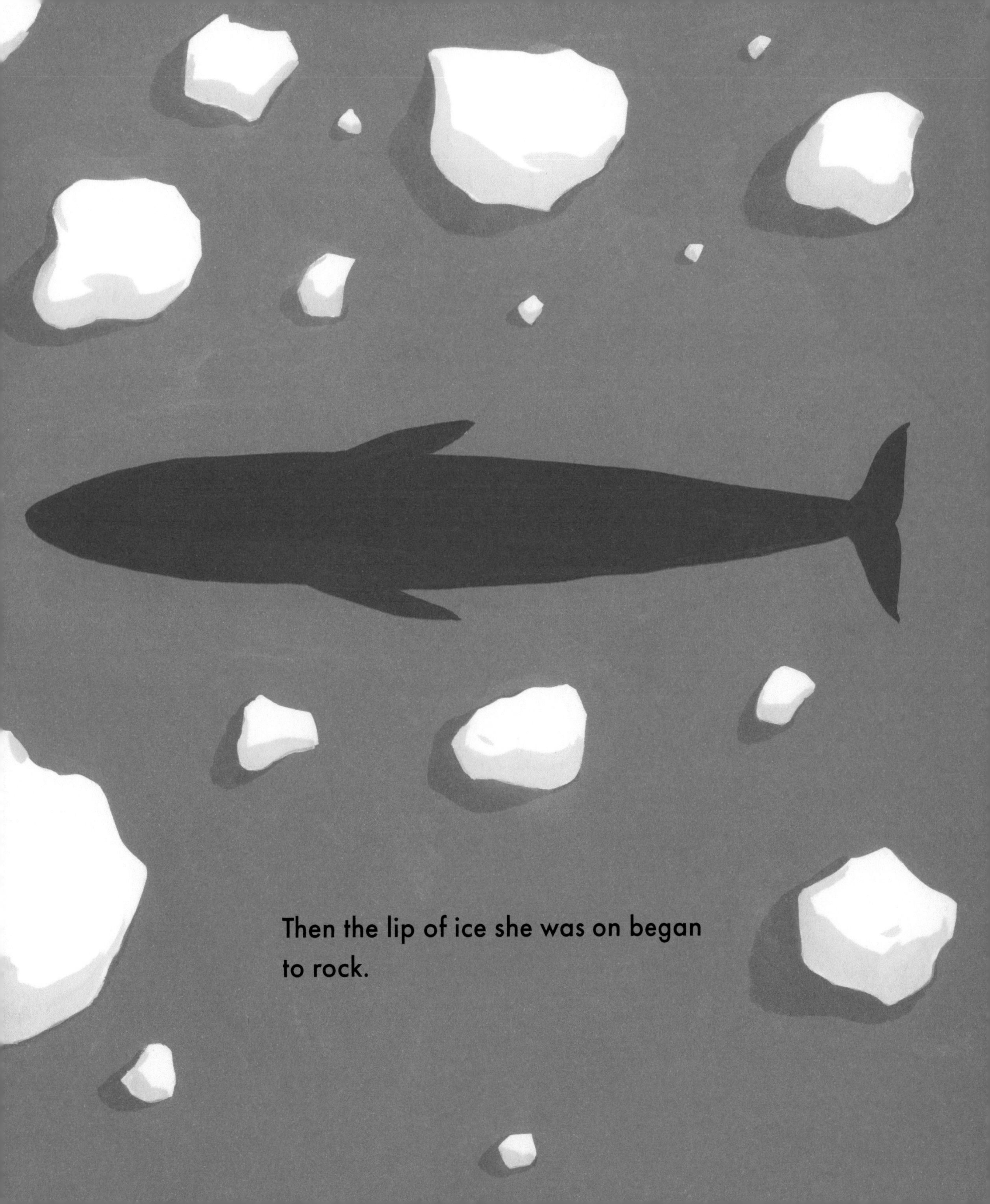

Then the lip of ice she was on began to rock.

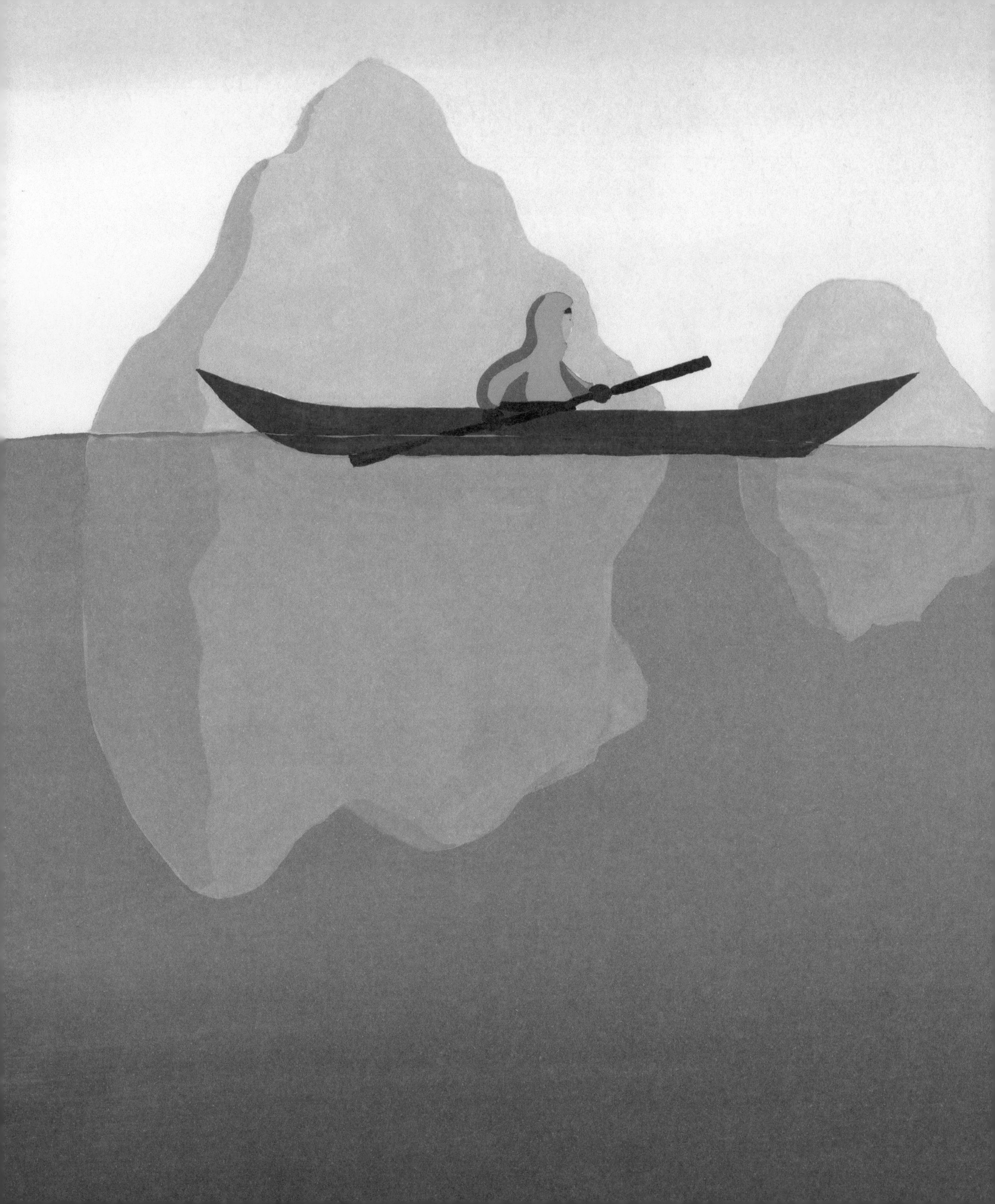

When Aia looked down,
she gasped in surprise.

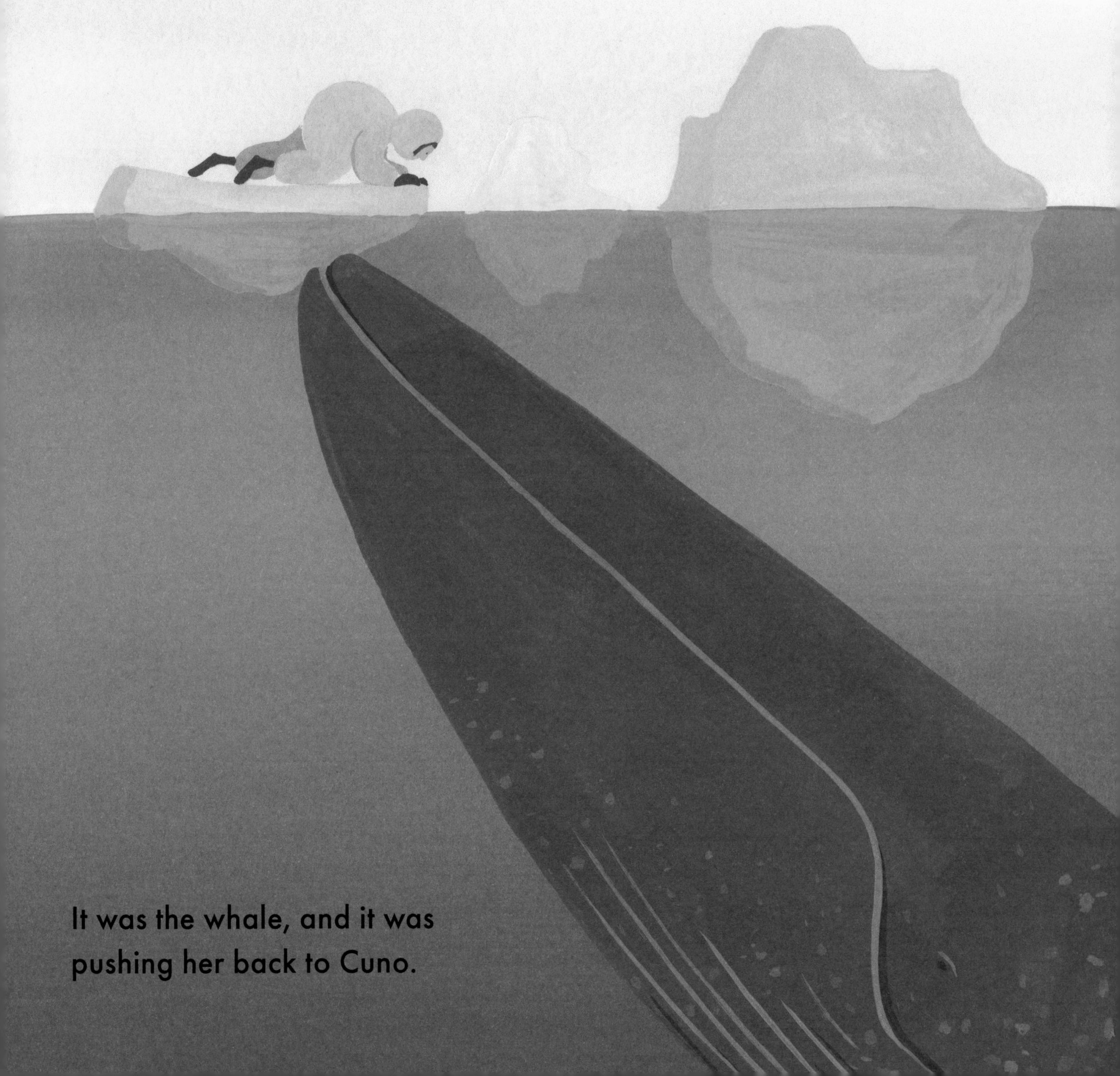

It was the whale, and it was
pushing her back to Cuno.

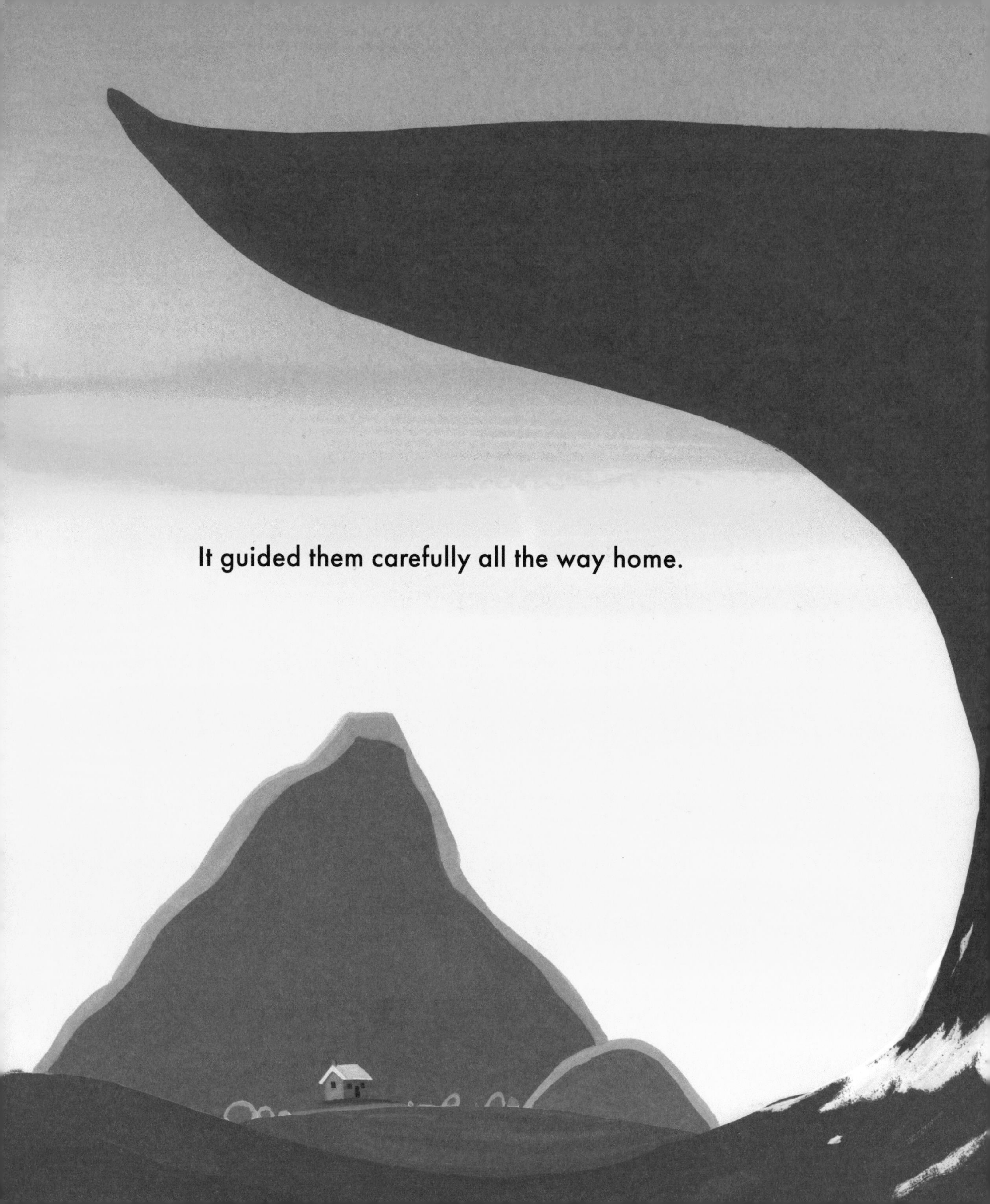

It guided them carefully all the way home.

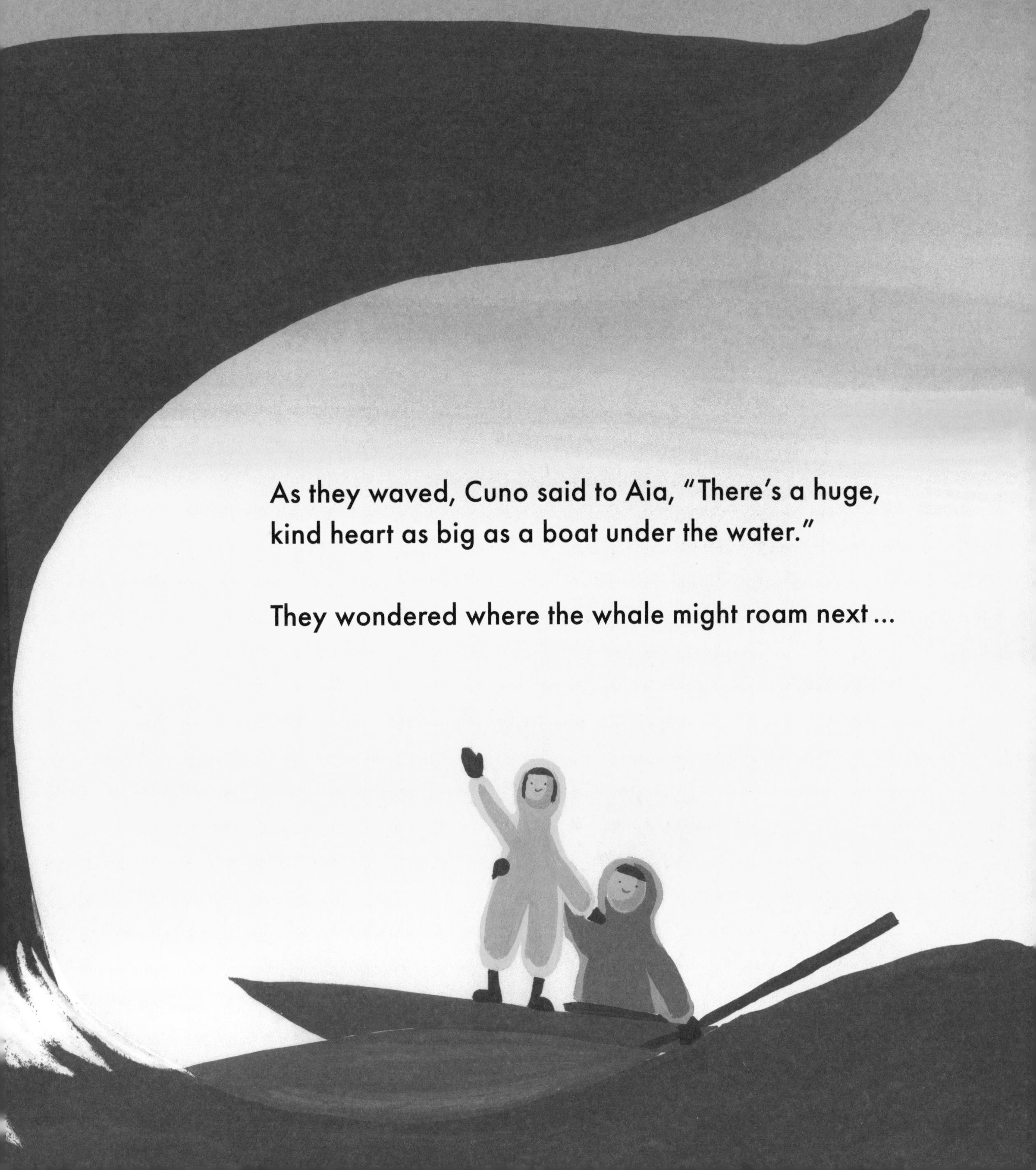

As they waved, Cuno said to Aia, "There's a huge, kind heart as big as a boat under the water."

They wondered where the whale might roam next ...

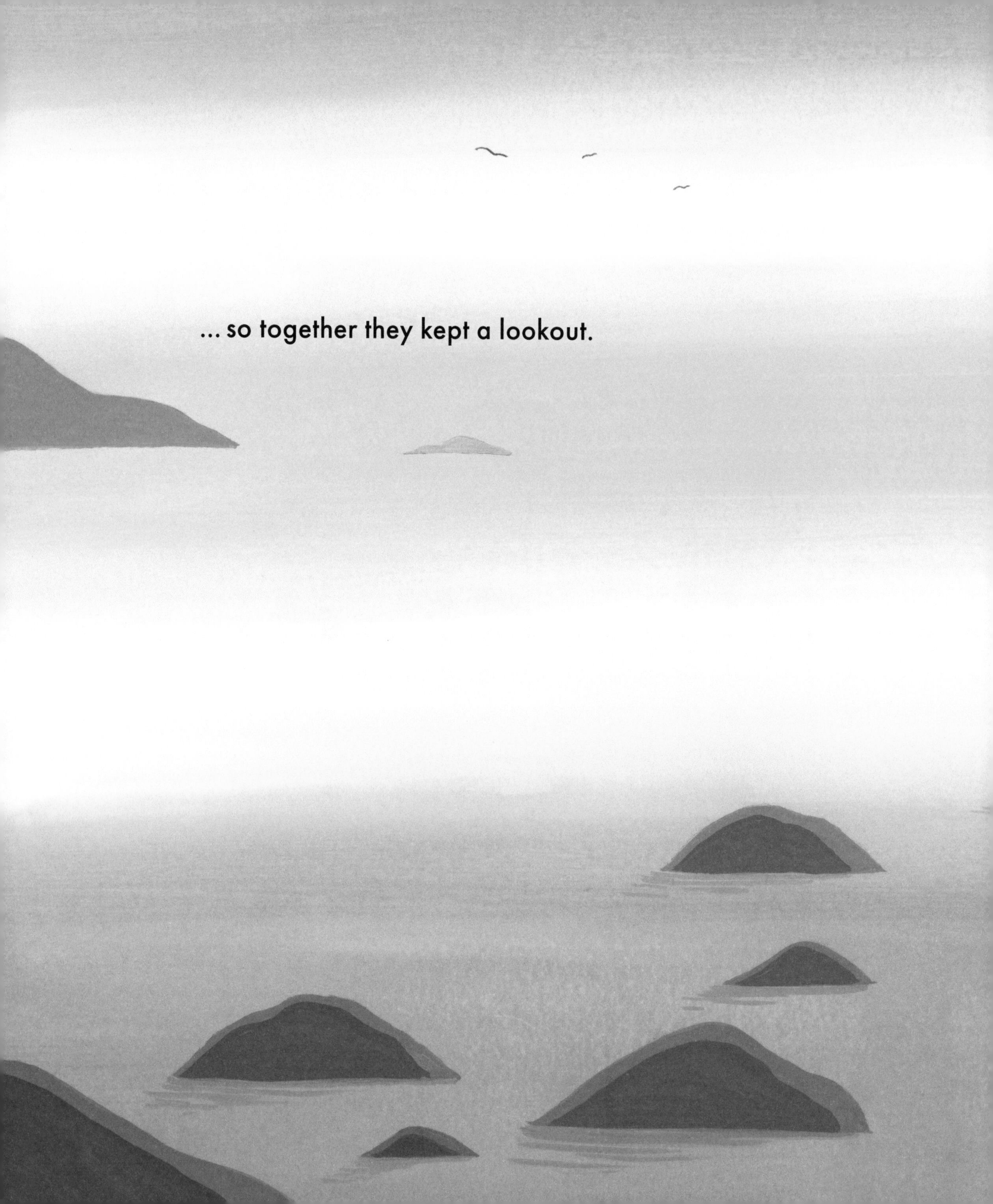

... so together they kept a lookout.

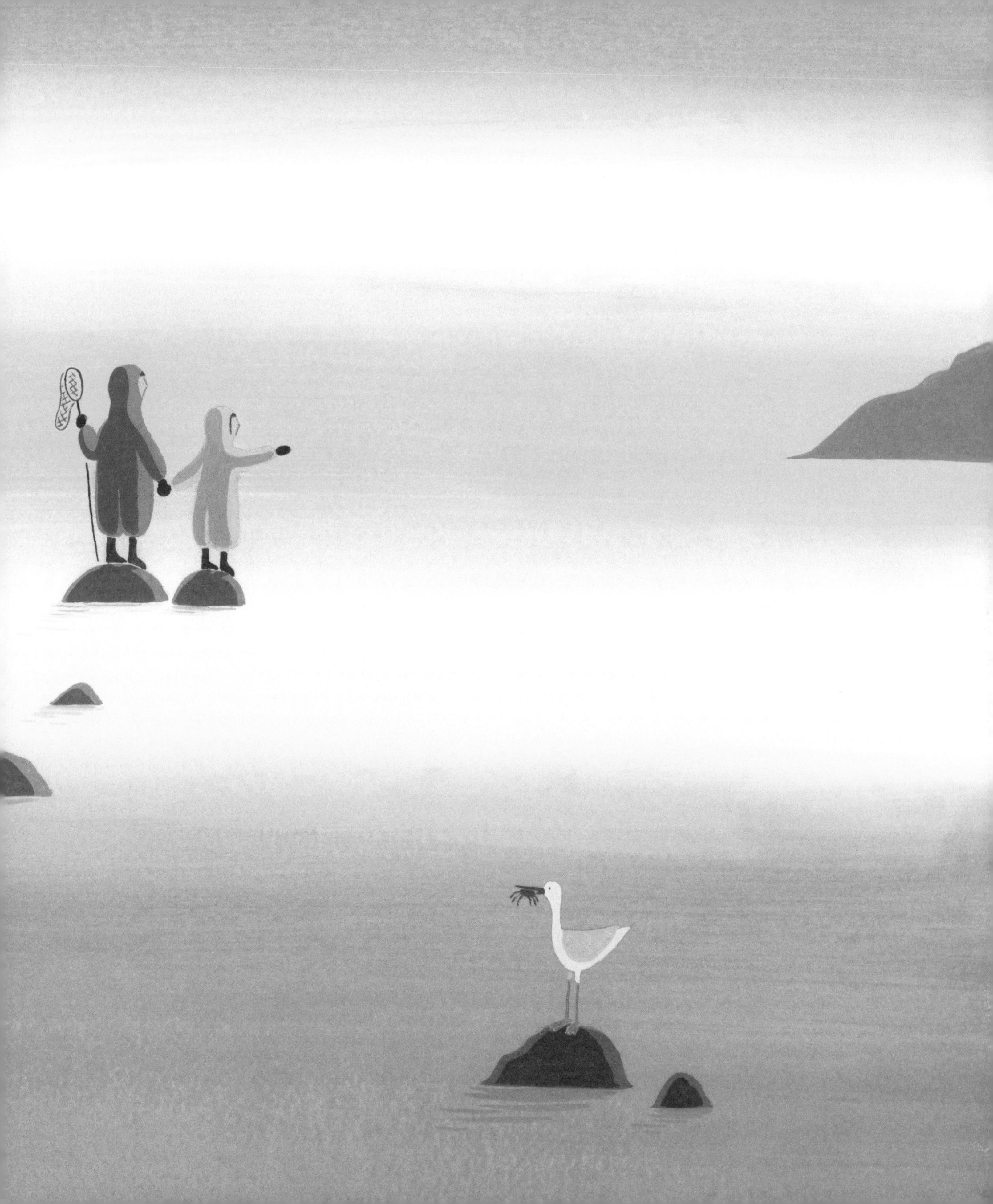

The Children and the Whale

Illustrated and written by Daniel Frost

This book was edited and designed by Gestalten

Edited by Robert Klanten and Angela Sangma Francis
Design and layout by Jan Blessing

Typeface: Futura PT by Isabella Chaeva and Vladimir Yefimov,
based on the original Futura design by Paul Renner

Printed by Grafisches Centrum Cuno GmbH & Co. KG, Calbe (Saale)
Made in Germany

Published by Little Gestalten, Berlin 2018
ISBN: 978-3-89955-816-6

The German edition is available under ISBN 978-3-89955-815-9

© Little Gestalten, an imprint of Die Gestalten Verlag GmbH & Co. KG, Berlin 2018

For more information, please visit little.gestalten.com.

Bibliographic information published by the Deutsche Nationalbibliothek:
The Deutsche Nationalbibliothek lists this publication in the Deutsche Nationalbibliografie;
detailed bibliographic data are available online at dnb.d-nb.de.

This book was printed on paper certified according to the standards of the FSC®.